The Wicked Uncle

Annie Woodward

Sequoia
PRESS AUSTRALIA

ISBN: 978-1-7635763-1-5

To all of the remaining Warner Brothers, but particularly Uncle Dick, who died in 1914, persecuted by the city he loved despite a lifetime of legendary generosity.

Preface

In 1986 builders working on a demolition site in Hackney discovered a leather briefcase wrapped in hessian, in a wall cavity.

A silver framed photograph of two girls was attached to the case with the inscription: The Elliot Twins, 1912.

Inside the briefcase were five undated journals composed in small, elegant copperplate handwriting that ran precisely between narrow margins. My grandmother, a historian, bought the briefcase at auction planning to research its contents.

She could not decide whether it was fiction or memoir. She tried, unsuccessfully, to substantiate the identity of the author. One fact she learned was that human remains had been found at the same demolition site, but never identified.

Before she died, my grandmother entrusted the mystery to me. I decided to edit the stories and leave readers to discover the truth.

The Elliot Twins

1
The Wicked Uncle

In 1911 life took a bitter turn when my guardian, James Parmiter Marriot, arrived home suddenly from India. He had been absent for so long that I presumed he was dead. If he had looked respectable, it would have been different, but he was not the sober, gentle young man I had once known. His return was also unsettling because I was no longer a little child. In his absence, my horizon had filled with musical education, and the joyous pageantry on the streets of London. The coronation of King George and Queen Mary was only six weeks away. My favourite conductor, Edward Elgar, was composing a coronation anthem. We had a street party planned, and an excursion to inspect modern innovations at the Festival of Empire. We had tickets for the pantomime *The Yellow Dwarf,* which was said to be a triumph for its costumery and mechanical sets. James was a frightening sight, a crippled, angry man on our doorstep on a cold Saturday, looking like a drunkard. He had power over my money and my plans, but I did not intend to be swept away from my cosy life. He did not resemble my mother's cheerful young brother who had tramped the meadow with me, long ago, awakening curiosity to the natural world. I quickly discovered that his decline was tragic enough to usurp the compassion of the people who had loved me in his absence, my uncle, Professor Angus Elliot, and his aunt. They were radical socialists, people with moral principles so intense that I should have guessed they would seize James as a fresh cause, even if it inflicted experimental ideas on every child living at 55 Morning Lane. My life was in danger of becoming the classic dark fable of an orphan.

Angus Elliot was my piano teacher, and when my parents died, he added me to his chaotic household. I was his most promising pupil. Aunty was a feminist, but not a suffragette. This was a problem because we were occupying a safe house for the most militant suffragettes in England. Aunty was not interested in the vote because she said the first thing girls needed was a classical education. That did not include classical piano, which she regarded as the preoccupation of dilettante debutantes. Her views led to chronic conflict over education between Angus and Aunty. Angus had promised me that he would scuttle the priorities of his aunt, to ensure my musical ability was nurtured. I had reached fourteen and I thought I was finished with school. Unfortunately, the rescue of the lost and lame was a greater cause. James Parmiter Elliot became their project. Everyone seemed to be ignoring the fact that James knew a great deal about the drowning of my family in the icy waters of Colden Bridge.

Our vast home at 55 Morning Lane was sometimes also called *The Orphan House*, not because it housed some orphans, but because the property had no value for the landlord, who was my grandfather, Marriot. He made his fortune in real estate, particularly slums. This house had been cobbled together from a couple of old cottages, and its wandering roofline had lean-to sections with no consistent architectural design. The collection of people in the house was as fluid as the structure, far more interesting than the rigid ranks of my own family. Angus had taken in a girl called Agnes, who had been put out of the Clapton Orphanage for scandalous behaviour. Dull and sullen, Agnes was not a child, but neither was she an adult or a real maid, but she was held in limbo by Angus's opposition to the institution of servanthood. My family's old housekeeper, Dotty, who had been a foundling, also moved in, but even in old age she was unwanted and uninvited. Another genuine orphan, Pearl, and her great-grandparents, became part of the household. I never fully understood where the various occupants of Morning Lane came from. Although my uncle believed children should be both seen and heard, he did not believe we should be privy to information about the people swirling around us, except in the case of the Dotty the housekeeper. The whole neighbourhood heard his rows with her.

Angus was a widower with twin daughters, Fanny and Jess, who were a year younger than me. They were an enigma to most people, although their father regarded them as wondrously perfect. Fanny, my very best friend, was wild and creative. She was disobedient and insolent by my parents' standards, but these words were not in my uncle's vocabulary. Jess was mysterious. My mother had told me she was not quite right in the head. She wordlessly flapped her hands and twisted her hair, ignoring everyone, but once she was in bed at night, she sang in a sweet soprano voice that echoed through the house. Both girls had a condition. Fanny's condition seemed to be her perennial excuse for outrageous behaviour. So often, Fanny seemed to be malingering.

Every Saturday we four girls – Fanny and Jess, Pearl and me - walked out with Angus and Aunty, regardless of weather, to visit the museum, or the waxworks, galleries or even a respectable music hall. On the way home Angus always found parks where we could play and quarrel as we trudged through damp grass, screaming, and playing chase. We pushed one another on the swings, and roused Angus from the damp bench to send us flying even higher. Sometimes, when Aunty stayed home, my uncle led us into the worst streets of London where he talked to bearded old Jews about books and music. He had lived in a Jewish community when he was a musician in Leipzig, and he claimed to share their beliefs, which seemed odd, as he was a Scottish Presbyterian. He knew some Yiddish and German, and the men in skull caps liked his company. We lingered around the street stalls while he talked, and eventually we were given pennies to buy sweet buns filled with mincemeat that stained our mouths with grease and sugar. When we finally got home in muddied boots, our noses blue from the cold, we were exhausted but satisfied.

On that awful Saturday that James Parmiter Marriot appeared, we had dashed into Morning Lane, quarrelling over trifles. The heat of the house overwhelmed us immediately. My uncle loved modern inventions. We had a coal-burning German combustion stove that was often hot enough to make its iron belly glow. We tore off our coats and mufflers and hats, abandoned our boots, and dashed away leaving an untidy trail that provoked Mrs Lloyd to follow, tutting mildly and retrieving garments. Mrs Lloyd was called our general factotum, to avoid any suggestion that she was the servant who cooked and cleaned. Pearl crawled onto the sagging couch under the stairs and fell asleep instantly in a nest of Aunty's knitted blankets, and Jess fell asleep in her own favourite place, against the banister rail, the fingers of her left-hand shoved deep into her mouth, the fingers of her right hand winding her hair into knots. Then Angus announced he would give Fanny a lesson at the piano. He had a new song in her vocal range, but first, she had to play the melody. She resisted his attempts to make her read music. It was such a simple task that I could not understand her stubborn refusal.

"Surely not on Saturday," Aunty muttered. It violated her rule of quiet Saturday afternoons. I watched resentfully as Fanny began wailing her excuses as she followed her father into the studio. Angus transformed into the professor as he walked through the door of his studio. It was the only place where he spoke sternly enough to persuade us that he expected to be obeyed. Fanny was the only pupil who did not comply. Within minutes Fanny had banged the piano lid shut twice, shouting a protest at her father's repeated: "Pianissimo, pianissimo." Then she dashed through the piece like a galloping horse as Angus bellowed: "Rall, rall, rall." I heard him congratulate her, but nothing could fuel her flagging strength. Aunty came into the chilly atrium where pupils waited for their lesson. She smiled with a sympathetic tilt of her head: "I'm going up for my nap," she said. "I think Fanny is exhausted today, and I don't know why your uncle persists in trying her strength."

"It won't last long," I said. "He wants to practise with me."

"Really? On a Saturday?"

"Saturday silence is your rule, not his," I said.

"Are you going to have one of those lessons where he shouts?"

"He doesn't shout at me," I said defensively. "I have to be able to hear him over the two pianos."

"Two pianos," she sighed. "One is too many on any Saturday. Can you remind him of our quiet Saturday afternoon rules?"

I was about to remind her, again, that it was not Angus's rule, but as she went up the stairs, I heard Fanny's familiar whine: "I am tired. I feel quite ill. I need to lie down."

Fanny's complaints wearied me, even if it did mean that I would soon get her father's complete attention. She had been learning to play longer than me, and she played competently by ear, but she refused to practise. I waited for her to flounce out of the studio, but instead, I heard an unfamiliar noise at the front door. Just when it seemed the bell would ring, there was a dreadful howl, the clatter of timber, the thump of bones on the icy stone, and gasps of pain. Annoyed at the possibility of an intrusive music pupil, I dashed through the atrium to wrench open the red door. There was no one on the steps, but I looked down, astonished to see a small man on his back on the icy pavement, looking like a toppled tortoise, a tangle of sharp limbs flailing. His pale, outraged countenance glared up at me. I went down and offered him my hand, but he flinched.

"Do not touch me, girl," he roared. "I can get up."

He obviously could not. I retrieved a broken cane and its runaway gold cockshead top and retreated to the door. He was struggling to use a second stick to regain his feet. His gloveless left hand was clawed. He dragged himself to the lowest step, one leg stuck out at an acute angle. It was so undignified. His knuckles were like clusters of marbles and his fingers sloped away at right angles. No glove would fit those hands. The lack of a topcoat was hard to fathom. Then I decided he was a Californian because his complexion had a touch of the sun, and perhaps London's chill had surprised him.

"Are you the American engineer we have contracted to install an elevating lift?" I asked, hoping to sound well-informed.

"Do I look like an American?" he asked.

I blushed at my mistake. As he reached the second step it occurred to me that I could circumvent a futile journey by enquiring again about his business.

"Are you sure you have the correct address?" I asked.

"Do you know who lives here my girl?" he retorted.

"I do," I replied hesitantly.

"There is no need to state the obvious, you blithering idiot. What name, girl?"

"I'm Kate Elliot," I said firmly.

When he heard my name, his limbs came to rest. He was rude by any standards, but the way he stared was fearful. He poked his stick at the small plaque over the letterbox, *Professor Angus Elliot,* to indicate he knew perfectly well where he was, and who he wanted to see. I felt humiliated by his arrogance.

"Are you Kate Elliot?" he demanded.

"Yes," I said hesitantly.

"Sir," he said. It took me a moment to realise he was correcting me. I was bewildered by the authority of this pathetic little man, instructing me from his knees at the threshold of my uncle's house. Was he not embarrassed by his infirmity? He hooked his arm under his knee again and drew himself up to the third step, almost at my eye level.

"You look about nineteen," he gasped. "My God you are the spitting image of Angus Elliot."

I had always been accused of resembling Angus. It was a point that baffled me and mortified my uncle, particularly as neither of his daughters had his red hair and long limbs.

"What are you doing opening doors?" he asked.

"I thought you were going to ring."

"Still no servants here?"

"Opening a door is not beneath me," I replied.

His knowledge of my family's plain life annoyed me. I stepped back each time he advanced, until I was inside the atrium once again. When he reached his full, unimpressive, height, I looked into his dull eyes and saw something familiar. I was about to admit my recognition just as he sneered: "Ah you've been well indoctrinated. Surely you know who I am?"

I refused the evidence of my memory. It was not possible that this was my other uncle, my guardian, home from India. It could not possibly be James Parmiter Marriot. The one I remembered was boyish, agile, kind, smiling and softly spoken. This was a cruel imposter.

"Professor Elliot is busy teaching," I said, pleased to emphasise the status of my true uncle. In the presence of this man, Angus seemed saintly, despite my concerns about his age, his religious obsessions, and his frustrating disregard for the important details of our lives, such as our education and his need of a wife. Angus, for all his faults, was preferable to this nasty little man.

"I will wait," he said.

He lowered himself gratefully onto the bench in the atrium, tired by his effort to shuffle the last few paces. I went to the far end of the bench and let my feet swing back and forth, wondering what I should do with him. He patted a clean handkerchief around his jawline and then began blowing at his nose. He tried to refold the muddied and bloodied handkerchief, his claw working against his thigh. His legs looked fleshless under his wide trousers.

I picked up some sheet music, abandoned by a pupil, and studied the interesting quavers ascending. I was turning my mind back to the problem of the visitor when a thunderous crash shook the walls, followed by a piercing high-e wail from Fanny.

"Noooooo. I hate you."

Three more dull thuds followed rapidly, the piano lid, the piano stool, the music stand.

"Sounds like bloody murder going on in there," the stranger remarked. "Someone's getting it. Are you waiting your turn?"

"Yes, I am," I said.

He studied me again, glancing from the music to the studio door. "I would run for it if I was you."

I put my head down further and tried to ignore him. Suddenly, he let out a blast of exasperation and demanded: "Can I go inside somewhere that's warmer? For God's sake Kate I am your uncle,

James. Have you forgotten me entirely? Were you not expecting me?"

At that moment Fanny, red faced and tear stained, bolted out of the studio, her hair wild. She bounced up the stairs calling out for my moral support.

"I'm here," I called back.

Fanny crouched down to look back to the atrium. Blotting her tears on her sleeve, she came back sedately to take a closer look at the stranger, staring at his crippled limbs. Her eyes glinted with morbid pleasure and feasted shamelessly on the spectacle, her mouth widening, lips pursed with contempt and curiosity.

"It's Uncle James," I said, to satisfy her intrusive gaze.

"Hello Uncle James," she said loudly, as though he might also be deaf, "I'm Fanny."

"I don't believe I am your uncle," he replied sharply, equally loudly, his eyes travelling with disapproval from her disorderly topknot to her stockinged feet.

"Kate and I are double cousins, so you would be my uncle," she said, freshly energised by the presence of a new object for gossip.

"I would not be," he said sternly. "I am your father's cousin."

"There, you see, you must be my uncle," Fanny retorted victoriously, certain she had proved her point.

"You are second cousins," I said. I was always disappointed that Fanny did not understand these conventions.

"You are at best a second cousin," James confirmed. "And as you are too young to call me by my Christian name the best I can suggest is you call me Mr James."

Fanny would not be put in her place by a stranger. She flipped her hair with the back of her hand and danced back into the studio to shout the information at her father: "Your cousin James is here. He says he is Katy's uncle. I thought you were. Make up your minds, I say. He's not my uncle, but I don't like him anyway."

Angus came to the doorway with three pieces of an ornate silver music stand that he was screwing back together. "I beg your pardon?"

By the time he glanced up to wonder about the content of Fanny's last volley, James was on his feet trying to be tall. Angus extended his elegant hand.

"Ooo you're cold," Angus said, patting the deformed hand he had just grasped weakly. "Kate, why didn't you take James into the parlour? He's freezing."

My uncle's other perfectly formed hand rested on James's shoulder and attempted to propel the invalid forward. James stumbled, steadied, and tried to smile.

"Fell on your steps, Gus," he said. "They need some ash or salt, whatever people put on them these days."

"Goodness, how dreadful, I must do something about that. Are you injured?"

"No, I am perfectly well. I can manage."

"You seem injured."

"This is me, Gus. Rheumatics," James bellowed. "London is so bloody cold that it makes it so much bloody worse. I haven't adjusted, yet, to this bloody cold and it is not even bloody winter."

"Boody terrible," Fanny said, laughing. She ran off as soon as she saw her father's grim expression. The six paces to the parlour were going to be a marathon.

"What an astonishing surprise James, after all these years," Angus said, ensuring he remained half a pace behind the invalid.

"I did send a calling card," James insisted, dragging a leg. "I'm living up the road, now, at the Parmiter place. No one came up to see me, so I came down."

My uncle's mystified eyes met mine. Neither of us could imagine what Mrs Lloyd would do with a calling card, because she could not read. At last, the invalid completed the journey and dropped into a straight-backed chair. He bent down to haul one knee over the other, and sat back exhausted, his stick sliding away from the chair. For a moment I thought the stick would be better housed outside with the umbrellas, but when I moved towards it, he said to me ferociously: "Leave it." I backed towards the wall, cowering at the rasping of his voice.

"I must apologise for my daughter," my uncle said quickly.

"Do you have to do that often – apologise for her behaviour?"

"No, Kate rarely forgets her manners," he said firmly, his smile fixed. "She must have been so surprised to see you. Kate's hospitality is usually impeccable. She is a little trooper."

I went and sat uncommonly close to Angus, as it seemed to be the only safe place.

"I was referring to your own girl. Is that the one with the condition?"

"Well then, I apologise for Fanny," Angus said abruptly, annoyed. "We have done badly on hospitality. What can I get you?"

"I could murder some tea."

"Ahhh...Kate, would you mind?" Angus asked.

I jumped up, anxious to escape.

"Make sure you come back because I came to see you," he shouted. "Are you training the little trooper as a maid, Gus?"

"Making a pot of tea is not beneath anyone living in my house."

"You've been inculcating your principles," he said cynically. "The old Orphan House looks somewhat improved. It's not a bad bit of property with some paint on it – a few knick-knacks and a couple of new chairs. Carpet underfoot. Quite domesticated. What has happened here, Gus? Men generally live in their wife's house. Have you married again?"

"No. But it needed a woman's touch. Philly Oroton helped me."

"Does that woman still have her hands in our pockets?"

When I returned, James continued to remark contemptuously on everything he saw. He contradicted every pleasantry Angus offered. Mrs Lloyd sailed invisibly through the parlour with cake, taking the measure of the visitor and communicating her assessment to me with a fractional movement of one eyebrow. Angus called these signals domestic politicking. He despised them heartily. I appreciated any hint of judgement, because Angus was invariably polite, and nothing he said endorsed our opinions of people.

James turned his attention to me again. “My father says this one is *in-ter-est-ing*.“ His misshapen finger waggled at me, and I wondered if he was trying to be humorous. “My sisters, of course, were brought up to be quite useless. This one reads, according to her grandfather. He sent me clippings from the trade rags about some examinations she passed.”

“Kate has passed her bronze and general proficiency at the Royal Academy, and she has won two major prizes for piano and violin. Perhaps she could play for you.”

“I’m tone deaf.”

“Yes of course, I had forgotten.”

“So, she’s a tinkler? My father said she was conversational. High praise from the old landlord. I suppose any female who would talk to the old man would impress him."

"Kate finished her education as school dux," Angus added. "Of course, the competition in a Borough school is not intense, but Kate was a good scholar."

"Borough school? What depths are we sinking to? At least my father had the decency to send his own daughters somewhere respectable. I suppose he would not come to the party for this one?"

Angus said nothing, but his hand squeezed my shoulder to ensure I did not leap to the defence of my grandfather. James spoke in shards of glass that I had to digest. The room was icy, as though someone had opened all the windows to allow winter to come inside. Stalactites were crowning me. I had become a sideshow curiosity to be mauled by this unpleasant man. Angus was polite and benign with most people, but I ached for some opposition to this rudeness. I knew he would not defend me. His political pacifism was rooted in a conciliatory nature. James pressed on with his sharp questions, but Angus volleyed every nasty observation, graciously.

"I was surprised that you volunteered to take this one in. I thought you found your own pair a bit of a millstone. Our Aunty wouldn't come to the party, then?"

"She is here. She lives with us. I could not manage without her. We both find children immensely interesting, and rewarding," Angus said firmly.

"I find them immensely annoying," James said laconically, using a claw to move the opposite arm forward towards the teacup that Mrs Lloyd had placed carelessly on a flimsy three-legged cane table.

"But it's good you took Kate," James mused. "I could not see why anyone imagined it was my duty. I don't know what my father thought I could do, apart from give you some educational advice, which of course, I wrote you. At least you are familiar with the role of parent to girls. Is your other one still alive? They were both sickly, weren't they, your own daughters?"

"The twins are very well," my uncle said softly.

"And the affliction? What is it?"

"Entirely unknown."

"The one I just saw is clearly not the mute."

"It is Jess who has no speech," Angus admitted.

"Is she deaf, Jess?"

"She can sing," I said. "She can sing contralto parts and even the Latin."

"Yes, but we need to explain that," Angus said quickly, anxious to avoid overstatements. "Latin is no more to her than English. Just collections of sounds. Basically, as James says, she is a mute."

This silenced James for a moment. He was perplexed by the information. He drank some tea and turned to me again. When he drew in his mouth to a pinch he looked like a foraging squirrel: "You have never answered my letters," he said, vehemently. "Girls are usually self-absorbed, but my father insists that, in your case, you have good handwriting, and you can string together some sentences in English quite competently. You really have no excuse for not writing."

"I must apologise," Angus began.

James held his hand up. "No, you must not apologise for what you cannot control. She is capable of apologising if she wishes."

I broke the pregnant silence abruptly: "I do not wish to apologise, Mr James. Your handwriting is illegible. How could I respond when I could not read a word you had to say?"

Angus made a long hissing sound as his breath escaped between closed teeth. He rolled his eyes to the ceiling and consulted the picture rails for God's wisdom. I would tolerate a lecture later for the pleasure of speaking my mind. It seemed scandalous to me that a school master had such appalling penmanship. James Parmiter Marriot's mouth twitched like a rabbit, and I visualised long whiskers and tall ears on him, working in harmony. His eyes were like bayonets fixed on me, but there was a twinkle in his previously dull eyes.

"You may call me Uncle James," he said with exaggerated kindness.

"I will call you Mr James." I replied. "If that is what Fanny must call you."

"You are quite a little madam," he said. "You used to be a compliant child. Are all the young females of England allowed to speak to their elders like this, these days, Gus?"

"Well, James." my uncle sighed with a genuine smile. "We can all have some interesting conversations about the young people of England, now you are home. I am sure our aunt would enjoy that debate."

James gave a little harrumphing laugh. He had finished his tea, but he still had a great deal to say. He laid his teacup aside and launched into an exhaustive treatise on the contents of his unread letters, his time in India, the sea journeys and storms, the intolerable heat, the flight to the hills during the long steamy rains, the stubborn, obstreperous, intractable boys he had taught who plagued his heart and mind and wore down his good temper. I presumed that he was making excuses for his absence. He must have spoken for half an hour, without a single word of amusement. It was raw. His stories contained relentless pessimism and unmitigated condescension. There was no music in his voice, only bitterness, and as he spoke the room became darker and colder. I moved closer to Angus, until my knees leaned against his and he drew me in with his strong arm around my shoulders. I was grateful for the course my life had taken. For all their faults, Angus and Aunty had made a safe harbour for us all.

Finally, when James gave perfunctory thanks for the tea and struggled upright on his cane, I hoped he would plunge into the icy darkness and break the rest of his bones. I stayed in the parlour, listening as Angus's melodious voice generously guided James out: "I will go in front of you just in case there is ice. These are such steep steps. I must have them replaced. If you miss your footing, you will only have me to blame."

Once James was gone, we went into the studio and worked on melancholy movements in minor keys until supper time. Later, Angus tapped the side of the German stove thoughtfully and said: "The fire has gone out. Why on earth has this fire gone out?"

I knew it was James Parmiter Marriot, full of malice, who had stolen the warmth of our house.

"Please tell me that you won't let him take me away?" I asked.

"I'm keeping you here, believe me. I don't think he is coming to your rescue. His dreadful incapacity has brought him back."

2

The Company of Preceptors

Aunty once again conducted consultations on our education. She said school, for me, was not over. It had barely begun, because I had no Greek nor Latin, no botany, and no higher arithmetic. But everyone was conspiring against Aunty. Angus had nothing to say on the subject if I was busy and content with music. Fanny would not go to school without me, and she was happily disinterested in any kind of exertion. The truant officer had called at the door, but when he saw Jess, flapping and twirling, and he discovered she was Fanny's twin, he ruled them out of his book.

Aunty sent for school brochures. I studied the alluring pictures advertising magnificent architecture and proud libraries of schools as far away as Ireland and Melbourne, Australia. She read each response thoughtfully, making marginal notes for my uncle, which he did not read. Angus was in the full flow of his own work. His students, his choir and his orchestra were performing throughout London and the provinces throughout the summer. Examinations would begin in six weeks. His work as an examiner would take him to Birmingham and Liverpool, and he had to reschedule rehearsals and lessons. Although he wanted me to travel with him, the real need was to find time to rehearse Seamus, the pet pupil who came early and left late and begged additional instruction from Angus for the two-piano Mozart concerto they would perform. I was given Seamus to work with. He issued instructions and became peeved each time he missed an entry.

"Stop and start again," he demanded.

"No, don't stop. People are too ignorant to hear your incompetence," I told him.

"You are very imperious for a girl."

"You are getting my help free," I said.

He seemed to doubt my words, but we rubbed along unhappily for an hour every night. He was nervous and self-conscious, and I knew his disposition did not match his ambition to be a concert pianist.

Fanny decided we needed new frocks suitable for girls who were no longer required at school. She was so sure that her father would be excited by her plan for a social life, that she was offended when he laughed her off. My uncle rarely refused us treats, but panto's and the Lyons tea house fit within his principles and Fanny could not see the nuances. I was pleased with the practical frocks that had come out of Aunty's tea chest, reminders of her slimmer self. Glamorous frocks for dancing belonged to another world. Aunty was militantly opposed to females with romantic hankering for parties. Fanny's fantasies were the result of reading romantic novellas, according to all the adults. Yet frocks were only the half of it. Fanny was fantasising a wife for her papa. It was an interminable discussion.

Fanny decided our appeal for frocks should be addressed to Miss Po, who still managed my father's electric light company. Miss Po was thin and manly, but she wore smart clothes. Most of my relatives were shareholders in the company, and Miss Po liked to tell me that she controlled my legacy. Fanny imagined she could share that legacy. Miss Po lived above the company offices in Holborn, a building I thought I could find because I had seen a photograph of it emblazoned with our family names. Fanny also intended to persuade Miss Po that my houndstooth coat needed to be replaced with something more becoming. Miss Po had conscientiously supplied our pinafores and boots for school, but those items were plain and serviceable, made, like the coat, to last a lifetime.

It was market day when Fanny decided we should pursue her plan to find Miss Po. We set out as soon as Mrs Lloyd left the house with her basket. When I worried out loud about this venture, Fanny claimed that the bible said it was wiser to apologise than ask permission, which was why we left Aunty dozing, ignorant of our movements. It was turning into a dark day. A dense carpet of black fog hovered just above the rooflines, obscuring light. I tucked my plaits under my beret so that I looked like any working girl waiting for a bus. We were grinning at one another excitedly, until we saw the queues of humanity going to work. We would have to walk. It must be an easy walk, I suggested, because Miss Po never paid fares on her journey from Holborn to Morning Lane. Fanny, however, was not convinced. We had only gone a hundred yards when she halted, and her arm became heavy in mine. I examined her pale face. All the ramifications of going to Holborn swarmed about in my brain. It was beginning to rain.

"Did you eat breakfast?" I asked.

"Yes. I had an egg. But I can't do this on foot," she said miserably.

We stood indecisively, watching people rushing by, locked up alone in their worries amid the great crowds. The roads were boiling with traffic, and there was a deafening wall of noise from motors and trams. The gutters were awash with debris. Wet heaps of horse dung were being splashed dangerously close to young men who were navigating the kerbside on foot or wobbling along the cobblestones on bicycles. Clothing was more colourful than it had been even a year ago, alive with splashes of blue and gold between the greys and beiges. Aunty had drawn our attention to fashion with her interpretation that it was evidence of coronation hope, prosperity, and a new era for the empire. On the inside of the pavement, young women in hobble skirts were constrained to small steps as they raced along on high heels, protected by the phalanx of anonymous men. The women were burdened with umbrellas, fur stoles, big muffs, and embossed leather bags. The speed of people was fearful. Even the old artisans in peak caps seemed to be moving fast, hauling their bulging Gladstone bags in various shades of decay. Men coughed and spat globs of green mucus into the gutter. There was an occasional shout of protest at a crowded bus, or a bellow at an agitated horse, but most people had their heads down, silent.

It was a tailored grey coat, new and expensive, that caught my attention. I would have preferred a darker colour on such a small man. Its wearer was lurching along on the far side of the road, with people resentfully gridlocked around him. It was a drunken stagger, two slow steps and a totter of three or four smaller ones, pitching precariously left and right, his arms thrusting about to achieve balance. His limbs seemed to be controlled by a puppet master who had tangled the strings.

"Is that Mr James?" Fanny asked incredulously. "Please do not look at him. I am too embarrassed."

I could not look away from the pathetic figure. Just as we were sure of his identity, someone pushed impatiently past him, and he pitched forward and rolled across the pavement. A dozen men kicked out as they stumbled around him, shouting obscenities. He lay motionless on the wet pavement. One ruffian took careful aim with his hobnailed boot and kicked him in the ribs. His Homburg was already under horses' hooves. He made such a small heap that he could have been mistaken for an overturned dustbin.

"We have to go and help him," I said.

"No," Fanny shrilled. "What can we do? And anyway, he is drunk."

"Papa would expect us to help him," I said.

"You are such a goody goody. If we help him, we will get found out for going to Holborn."

"We haven't gone to Holborn."

"Haven't you learned yet that helping people always lead to trouble?" she asked.

"We must help him."

Fanny looked at me incredulously. I took her arm and propelled her towards the road, and drove her forward through the mud, straw and coal-dust to the safety of the kerb. James Parmiter Marriot was gasping aloud as he attempted to lift his face away from the ground.

"Can I help you get up?" I asked.

"Do not touch me, girl," he said.

"You need help," I said, astonished to meet him a second time in this position.

"Of course, I need someone to help me."

His abrasive voice was choked in pain.

"I am someone," I protested. "I am Kate. Do you remember me? I'm tall and strong and I can help you get up."

A man shouted: "Let him rot. No child should have to get their father out of the gutter."

Fanny folded her arms defensively, to assure me that she could not help.

"Leave me. Go and get Gus," he gasped. "It will take a man to carry me home."

"He is teaching at the university today. What about Old Nort? He lives at the back of Parmiter. He has a horse and cart."

"Yes. I know where he lives. I live there. Go and get him," he barked.

"Stay here, Fanny," I said.

"I cannot stay here alone," she said.

"You are not alone, Fanny," James croaked. "I am here."

She glanced down imperiously and thankfully she did not state the blithering obvious. She looked over the sad heap of tangled limbs, her chin pulled in like a disdainful old woman and folded her arms in defeat.

"Kate, go," he said.

I took off my hated houndstooth coat and laid it across James, tucked my scarf and bonnet under his head, and gave Fanny my purse. I then added to the nonsensical discussion by saying to James, "Please remain here until I return."

"I probably shall," he responded coldly.

I hitched up my skirt and ran along Clapton Road, weaving fiercely through the crowds of workers. I leapt over three paving stones at a time. When I reached Parmiter, I jumped over the iron railings and squeezed between the hedgerows to reach the back scullery where Mrs Nort was making soup. She looked up in surprise and grinned wordlessly, toothlessly.

"I want Mr Nort," I said.

"Och aye," she said vacantly.

"Mr James has fallen," I said.

She stared at me for a moment, the cogitations of her mind evident. Then she bellowed into the air, eyes locked on me: "Nort, Nort. It be the young Mr James hurt hisself. 'Eee be needin' thee."

Nort appeared in the doorway of the red brick water closet, his braces down, a sheet of newspaper between his lips, pinning his trousers back together.

"What's up'ee?" he asked calmly.

"We need the horse and cart," I said. "Mr James is on the pavement, hurt. He fell. At the junction."

Mrs Nort handed him his cap and coat.

"Och aye," he said, and gestured me to lead the way.

"What about the horse and cart," I repeated.

"Nay. Nay. I pick him oop," he muttered as he followed me briskly.

A small, more sympathetic crowd had now gathered around James, offering encouragement to Fanny who was advising complete strangers that it was her second cousin who had fallen, and he was not drunk but had a bad leg. She was holding his crippled hand between her thumb and forefinger, mid-air, in such a persuasive gesture of concern that she was winning the admiration of the audience. She looked up at me in great relief, rosy cheeked and immensely pleased with herself. Mr James was still insisting that no one should touch him. A couple of men were offering to get him on his feet, and one had slipped an arm under his shoulder so that James was pushed awkwardly forward, gasping with pain, his limbs too stiff to manipulate back into working order. Nort nudged gently through the crowd and wordlessly scooped him up. Grunts and gasps emitted from James's throat. The crowd chorused surprise at the old man's strength, and Nort trudged back towards Parmiter as though he was carrying a small sack of potatoes. Fanny and I followed with James's crushed hat, his broken cane, and the houndstooth coat now soaking wet and filthy with mud and coal dust, manure and spittle.

"You need a new coat," Fanny said triumphantly. "I put it on the path and about fifty people walked over it."

"Get my keys from my pocket," James told me.

I put my hands into every deep pocket of his coat and found nothing.

"I had my pockets picked the last time I fell," he said miserably. "Someone offers to lift you up and they lift everything you've got."

"Nort can take you through the scullery to your house," I said.

"No access. My father had it bricked off from the main house," James muttered. "Godsake, what was he thinking?"

"You can come to our house," Fanny said brightly. "It is nice and warm and later on we can push Agnes through a window to open your house."

This seemed like one of Fanny's more spectacular solutions and Nort was ayeing it all. Nort brought James into Morning Lane and lodged him on the chaise under the stairs, close to the German stove.

"Go and break a window to get into Parmiter, Nort," James said. "And let's get that wall knocked down at the back of the scullery. I need your help inside the house not locked out there."

At the sight of the wet and dishevelled visitor, Agnes tossed a blanket at the couch and galloped up the stairs for Aunty, who immediately made a miraculously agile descent of the stairs, wrapped in two silk shawls, and flushed with purpose. Aunty eased herself down into a wide chair that Mrs Lloyd brought out of the parlour. She was a portrait of charity and righteous indignation.

"Poor young Jim," she sighed. "You've got what my father had. We thought your side had escaped this thing, but it's come through to you, hasn't it?"

James turned a wan smile to her and nodded feebly: "Probably, Aunty. This is an unfortunate way to meet again. I had a fall, and I've have just been rescued by the girls on their way to school. My God young Kate can run like the wind on those long legs. Thank God they were there. What on earth were you thinking to let them walk out alone among commoners in this weather?"

Aunty turned her puckered mouth to us, eyes ablaze, full of promises of further discussion.

"Girls," she said in a honeyed tone, "We need some hot tea, because poor young Jim is trembling with the cold. Agnes, go and get some dry trousers and a Guernsey from the Professor's cupboard. I do not want you moving, Jim, because you have had a terrible tumble."

"Yes, well I was given a rather good push," he said defensively. "But when I get like this in the cold, I seize up."

"Dreadful," Aunty sniffed, "London people are so ignorant."

He surrendered entirely to her ministrations. We brought the tea, and Aunty skilfully peeled off the wet outer garments and boots, slipped his twisted limbs into my uncle's socks, and jersey, and tucked his legs into mounds of pillows. She drew a blanket up to his chin and wrapped it over his shoulders, and then deftly tucked a bolster into the small of his back. James' body seemed to uncoil from its habitual tensions. Aunty helped him with his tea. It was curious to watch this bad-tempered man surrender to her gentle concern.

"I nursed my father for years," Aunty said, mostly to satisfy our curious stares. "You have to stay warm and still until this tension passes."

"Yes," James concurred.

I poured her tea and placed it in her lap and went in search of a biscuit. Pearl and Jess came down to watch the proceedings. As some colour returned to

James's cheeks, he looked around in amazement at the gathering crowd.

"Aunty, how many people live here?" he asked.

"Just Gus and his four girls and myself," she replied. "And the general factotums of course."

"Four girls," he repeated. "Four?"

"This little one is Pearl. I think you know the others."

She stretched her hand towards Pearl, and the little girl stepped forward fearlessly to inspect the visitor. Her skin was radiant, and her golden ringlets fell down her back in uniform rows. We knew her beauty was irresistible, and she was a source of pride to us all, but we did not expect this odd little man to be so thoroughly undone by her charm. A flicker of humanity crossed his face.

"What a lovely, delightful child. Where has she come from? Is she Gus's child?"

Aunty said thoughtfully, "She is now, and therein lays a tale."

We were not allowed to hear Aunty tell her tale, because we were sent upstairs to dry ourselves off. I was interested in James's response to Pearl. On this encounter he was less monstrous, and more an object for pity.

Glowing with our own goodness we were confident our unapproved excursion would be eclipsed by the saga of our rescue operation. What we did not imagine was the solution to Aunty's pressing dilemma – our education – was being formulated as the two adults enjoyed a reunion in the alcove under the stairs. They had discovered a common bond; they were both members of the College of Preceptors.

After James was safely returned to Parmiter, the College of Preceptors was announced several times throughout the afternoon, first to Mrs Lloyd, to Agnes, and then to a variety of piano pupils who listened in either confusion or dismay to Aunty's account of her ministry to James. She told them she was collecting a list of the names of their younger brothers and sisters.

"What are preceptors?" Fanny asked me.

Dr Johnson offered the impenetrable word *pedagogue* to explain preceptor. Later in the day, as we clustered around tea, my uncle supplied the definition. They were teachers who taught teachers. This fact had led to an appalling solution to our educational dilemma. I would become a pupil teacher. An aid to James. Aunty said she had simultaneously resolved the educational needs of Fanny, Jess and Pearl, not to mention James's need for an honest living. There was plenty of space in Parmiter for a school.

"The poor man, a member of the College of Preceptors, has been trudging around these poor London schools looking for a post," she said. "Of course, I could not say so to the poor man, but with his affliction being so severe, what chance does he have? He has the Cambridge mathematics tripos – a master's degree in fact - so of course he doesn't want charity from the landlord."

"What landlord?" Fanny asked.

"Uncle Marriot is the landlord," I said. "He's Mr James's father."

"Why do they call him that?"

"So that we don't know who they are talking about," I said.

"But I don't know who you're talking about. I thought Uncle Marriot was your grandfather. How can he be Mr James's father if he's not my uncle? Whose uncle is the landlord?"

Angus laughed, shrugging at me as though it was beyond explanation: "Marriot is my uncle," Angus said. "He is Aunty's brother."

Fanny made a wild gesture that indicated her mind was exploding, and she made her escape from the incomprehensible conversation.

"So, I said to James," Aunty said, determined to ignore the comedy, "Gus has perfectly good patrons, and he is only teaching them the piano. Music pupils have brothers and sisters in need of a proper classical education. Gus, you have built up a wonderful music school. Poor Jim, bouncing around in that house by himself. A big parlour begs for a good private school. And I can help him of course, it would be wonderful for me to teach Latin for a couple of hours each day. And, he had noticed how obliging and considerate and how helpful Kate can be, and so I said, Kate can help him."

"I think you might have asked me first," I protested. I looked at my uncle in alarm, waiting for the protection and support I thought he had promised me. He was flustered by his aunt's sudden enthusiasm and shrugged again, defeated.

"I told him all about you, Kate, and he could see that you are a responsible, intelligent girl capable of doing anything she sets her mind to. In need of a classical education," Aunty said. "He has a great mind. Kate, and you will make a most excellent pupil teacher for the younger ones."

"What about Fanny?" I asked.

"What indeed? I told James that you two are inseparable, one voice when there should be two, and a bit of divide and conquer would be required."

"Yes, yes, Aunt, but Kate is already teaching. She has her own beginners in piano, and not much time," Angus finally protested.

"And, dear Gus, you can have Jess in school as well. He is quite willing to take Jess as long as there is someone to manage her. And Kate manages her so well."

"I cannot believe you have taken my future in your hands without a by-your leave," I said.

"And what precisely was your plan, Kate?" she asked. "Running off on trams in the rush hour for goodness knows what purpose?"

Angus avoided my eyes. Aunty shared the minute details of her scheme. Everyone would come back home at dinner time and if it transpired that the afternoon was too long for Jess, or Pearl, or even Fanny, they would stay home for the afternoon, while I remained for my classical education, to prepare me to matriculate to London University, as there was no benefit for girls in going up to Cambridge or Oxford where they were not wanted. As she talked incessantly, she ate at an equal pace. I studied the way Angus approached his plate delicately, and I realised he was approaching the discussion just as cautiously. I waited for his questions, or objections, but there were none.

"It would be wonderful if Jess could go to school," he conceded. "And I do not want Pearl going to that rough school down the road, by herself, so young."

"Indeed. And Kate, what a wonderful opportunity to be trained to teach," Aunty said.

"I think it has all changed since your day, Aunty, and I am far too young to be anyone's teacher," I said.

"But you teach piano to little girls. There is no difference," she argued.

"There is a great deal of difference between a piano lesson that lasts half an hour and a whole day of teaching at school," I said.

"You will only be James's assistant. I won the prize called the Queen's Own Scholar when I was your age," Aunty continued, nodding at me gravely "It was a scholarship to be trained as a teacher. I flew in the face of my father to do it. The wonderful old queen herself did so much for women and children."

Angus tried to get away, and he remembered a pupil who might be waiting, but Aunty was not finished. Fanny returned for more cake, her eyes narrowed in accusation at me, as though I had designed the debacle. She shook her head dramatically and began groaning as Aunty described the wonderful egalitarian qualities of the old queen, who seemed to have been dead all our lives.

"I told you, Kate," Fanny whispered. "I warned you that helping people always leads to trouble. Haven't you seen the trouble papa gets himself into with lame ducks? I told you."

When Aunty finished her diatribe and went off to read with Agnes, Fanny unleashed her fury: "This is all your fault, Kate. You have brought so many strange people into this house, but this is the worst. What were you thinking to invite him here? You should have gone off to grammar school when you had a chance. I don't think we will be able to be friends if you are going to be a teacher. With HIM."

Angus was usually amused when Fanny spoke so dramatically, but he sat looking miserably into his tea leaves. He was defeated. Although I was impatient with his passivity, I knew Aunty had exposed a significant problem. We were a houseful of indolent girls squabbling all day long. I was constantly unravelling the girls' problems. Angus was agitated because his teaching schedule was disrupted by their demands. If there was an urgent upset, Aunty was not agile on the stairs, and she refused to raise her voice. The factotums would not resolve spats without direction from Aunty. At times, Pearl seemed intelligent, and she was so bored in the nursery that she needed to begin some formal learning. Fanny was immature and would not develop a life of purpose without better education. Anything we did for Jess was better than seeing her languishing on the stairs. I also wanted more education, as long as I did not have to abandon the piano, get on a bus, and play cricket in a short frock.

"It won't be worse than what you're already doing," Angus said quietly, with an unusual burst of insight. "We're going nowhere fast with the music curriculum at the moment, because you are basically doing nanny duties with naughty girls."

"It can organise the chaos," I admitted.

"I don't have to quarrel with Aunty, then?"

"It will probably be alright," I conceded. "As long as I am home in time to practise."

Just one week later we were ushered into the chill front parlour at Parmiter where a sad fire struggled for life in the grate. I had not been in the house for five years, and I began trembling and tears pricked at my eyes as I entered the room. My emotions shocked me. Parmiter had never been cold, dark and neglected. All my parents' elegant mahogany had been shoved under sheeting at the back of the room, the carpet rolled up, and the space was naked except for a cluster of new electric light bulbs gazing down dismally over a group of new children's desks There was not a gouge or inkblot to be seen on any desktop.

As the school day unfolded, I began to breathe more easily. I had not volunteered to become the assistant to a frightening invalid, but something about the appointment appealed to me. It was a seductive status that confirmed my cleverness. I was curious, quietly excited, and only dragging my feet a little. The idea of a school so close to home, and the opportunity for Fanny, Jess and Pearl to learn, persuaded me that it was a worthy task.

Six other children, recruited from among the families of studio musicians, joined us; the first of many children who stayed briefly, names and faces soon forgotten. The arrival of children gave me a weight of responsibility. The presence of Jess, silent and unteachable, and irrepressible Pearl, wiggling and dancing and anticipating my indulgence, worried me. Fanny, undecided about the enterprise, was at first sweet and compliant, just as she had always been in the Morning Lane School. She was evaluating her options, she said, but it was soon clear that she had none, and our friendship was under siege.

"This was your fault," Fanny reminded me grimly. "You have become like my father, being kind to complete strangers. And that causes trouble."

My dilemma was soon obvious. James would use his big voice to reach where he could not go. He wedged himself behind a standing desk that backed onto a wall, his slight weight resting on a tall stool. He could not move from that position, but his voice boomed fearfully across the floorspace. I was his hands and feet. His walking cane tapped with menace against the tall skirting boards, instructing me to scurry thither and yon on his behalf. By the time the girls needed their dinner, I was exhausted.

In private Fanny called him Poor Jim, mimicked his agonised gait, and imitated the way he spoke in a harsh rasp through an immobile mouth. The sinister aspect to his hard character was that he frightened the children, and sometimes, their mothers. It was not his physical limitations so much as his bluster, and the lack of kindness in his manner that offended people. I had glimpsed another dimension to him at Clapton junction. He sometimes saw life with something akin to my own cynicism, and a smirk crossed his face. Any humorous intent vanished so quickly that he was just a tyrant.

I was assigned to teach Pearl. He raised a nobbled finger and pointed it weakly towards Jess, and demanded: "What can that one do?"

"She can do puzzles."

"She will not do puzzles."

"She can sing."

"She will not sing."

"That is all she does," I said.

"Then you must teach her the alphabet," he said crisply.

"How will I do that?"

"You will use your initiative and imagination."

At night Fanny and I fell on our beds and agreed to hate Mr James unconditionally. When we tired of repeating the same complaints, I excited Fanny with my stories of Colden Bridge, where my brother, Cyril, drowned. Fanny encouraged me to retell my story and as I had no truth to tell, I wove speculation and assumptions from what I had overheard. I embellished. Each time I told the story, I loaded it up with the day's resentments so that it deviated into a fantastic tale of malevolence wherein James murdered Cyril. We laughed uproariously as the malice intensified over many nights. We knew it was fiction. At least, I did.

As more small children joined the school, Aunty loaded me with advice and ideas and estimated that this discharged her teaching duties. The mornings rushed by, and I felt a growing affection for my little charges and took pride in their progress. If James noticed my efforts, he gave no indication but sat silently preparing afternoon lessons for the older pupils. Fanny regarded these lessons as medieval torture. The abundance of books he introduced meant the afternoon expanded conversationally, following threads of information, pursuing new ideas. Even when he set a topic for an essay, it led me into rich seams of history, culture and philosophy. I could not hide my love of complexity and detail. When I asked questions, Fanny despised me.

I approached the teaching of the small children in a new way after I remembered that I had become an accidental reader by learning the letters of the treble clef at the age of four, sitting alongside Angus on the piano bench. I learned to count in the same way. I sang the letters to Jess, jumbled them, matched them, dangled them before her eyes Each day she rocked contentedly in her desk, fingers sucked to wrinkles, watching the letters of the treble clef assembled on a piece of card in front of her. Each day James would bark the same futile instructions.

"Take her hand from her mouth."

I did. She re inserted it deftly.

"And stop her rocking."

"I have tried."

"Try again. The singing is not working."

"But it is," I protested weakly.

"I see no evidence," he said coldly.

"We do." Fanny announced defensively.

James ignored her. No matter how frequently or loudly Fanny made her declarations on any topic, he averted his eyes and searched the floorboards, as though mice had scurried past, or beetles were creeping up through the cracks. He ignored her steadfastly throughout the day. In the afternoons there were five of us in his high school class, but he never called on Fanny for an answer, and never commented on her spontaneous comments. To be ignored was the most painful humiliation for Fanny, and she scratched the scab off that wound each evening when we were alone. The day ended with Fanny crying with frustration and anger. When I cornered Aunty alone to complain, she was dismissive: "Sometimes a teacher has to be cruel to be kind."

"Fanny is not well," I protested.

"I have cared for invalids all my life and they must be kept working. There are too many of these malingerers in society today, and Fanny has dithered and procrastinated for years."

"That is hard and cruel," I said. "I cannot believe you are siding with Mr James."

"I am on your side, Kate. You have too much promise to be held back by Fanny's nonsense."

James kept up the pressure on me to find ways to teach Jess. At home when I played the scale, she made a fair imitation of naming the notes. I believed she was trapped, locked within herself, simply unable to get out and into our world because language had no more meaning for her than for a cart horse.

"If I could unlock the piano," I suggested to James, "She might sing for you."

"I am tone deaf," he replied coldly, as though it resolved my dilemma. "I cannot abide the noise of people banging on pianos. I do not wish to have her sing to me. I want her to learn the alphabet so that she might read."

In time I was able to bring Jess's puzzles to class, and James watched, fascinated, as she assembled, scrambled and reassembled the puzzles repeatedly. I turned over the coloured pieces so that no picture was evident, and she rapidly fitted them back into a whole. He watched her matching shapes, matching colours, pouring sand cautiously from one cylinder to another. He was impressed by her ability to signal her needs for the lavatory or a drink, to follow the instructions to sit, stay and come. She had also learned to manipulate her own clothing. He made copious notes of his observations.

"She is not entirely an imbecile," he informed me. "But unfortunately, Gus has just trained her like a dog."

Six months after the parlour school began, as the other pupils were singing the entire alphabet, Jess's small soprano voice rose over them, perfect pitch, but inarticulate. I was kneeling near two five-year-olds, who were pointing to their letters as the song progressed, and from the corner of my eye I saw James was alert, full of wonder. When I looked up, his face hardened.

"Twenty-six letters and you only wanted eight," he said. "She is now ready to read."

Jess's alphabetical triumph led to celebrations around our breakfast table. Fanny, Aunty and Mrs Lloyd were impressed. Only Angus was philosophical.

"That singing skill is not really new to us, is it?" he asked. "Did she clearly articulate?"

"Of course not. But Mr James thinks she is ready to read," I said. "He doesn't understand her at all."

"He is just very optimistic. Don't speak of him so harshly."

"He said you trained Jess like a dog," I told him maliciously.

He flushed, his face steaming with indignation and offence. He tried to contain his anger as he complained to Aunty: "I had no other way of managing Jess at the time. It sounds appalling, but it certainly worked. I regard that as an unwise betrayal on James's part, breaking my confidence, repeating my words to my children."

"Not wise," Aunty said sympathetically. "You kept Jess out of institutions, and she is well trained for a child of her capacity. James is just a young man, Angus. He doesn't understand the real trials of training children."

"It does not demonstrate any integrity. I shall be very cautious in what I say to him in the future. I am so disappointed."

His words were wonderfully harsh, and I hoped that was a blight on their friendship.

The American engineers finally came to build the elevator. It was not as disruptive as earlier renovations. Within a week the lift was shuddering up and down, and the builders went away satisfied with their ingenuity. Everyone was delighted that the new contraption had eliminated the steep back stairs and absorbed another box room on a landing that had accommodated mice and wardrobes full of old clothes. Fanny was fascinated by the mountains of moth-eaten frocks pulled out of the disused room, and she wanted to keep them for dressing up. Angus said it was all Uncle Marriot's rubbish that should have been removed a decade ago: "Just burn the lot," he told the housekeeper. Nort carted everything off for a bonfire. Once it was dark we went out with the general factotums to watch. We spent the evening at the fire, laughing uproariously as we took turns to first try-on some garments, and then toss them into the fire. There were whalebone stays, petticoats and hoop skirts that crackled ferociously in the flames, a moth-eaten livery, strange bonnets, a cat of nine tails, some knives and swords of papier mâché, and some fur wraps that were still attached to beady eyed fox heads. Later, Aunty confided in me that when she saw us dancing about in the big, bright dresses, she realised they were theatrical costumes that probably belonged to Fanny's mother.

Once Angus declared the elevator open for business, Aunty refused to use it. Angus enticed her into the small iron cage with his reassuring banter, but she sat apprehensively on the edge of the wooden bench for the ascent, her timorous squeals suddenly giving way to a single blood curdling scream of terror, fading in and out of earshot, as the machine shuddered up through the wall cavity. Fanny and I sped up the stairs, following the fading cry. As the cage was opened, she shuffled out white and trembling, shaking her head vociferously: "No, no, oh no, no, no, Angus, it is unnatural. It cannot be good for me. It is a terrifying contraption. It cannot be safe."

At that moment I felt age had eclipsed her fighting spirit, and I watched in great disappointment as she dragged her bad leg slowly towards her room, batting us all away.

Fanny and I took charge of the machine and happily transported bed linen up and down on behalf of Mrs Lloyd, who was equally afraid of the cage. Our less essential elevations were restricted to those times when my uncle was out. Despite Jess's terror of motorised transport, she seemed to enjoy the lift. Pearl also delighted in it, although she took her lead from Aunty and screamed all the way up and down, drawing the unwanted attention of her nanny, so that we often left her in the nursery. We took turns yanking the lever, ringing the bell, opening and closing the cage, and standing on the seat so that we could see precisely where we were in relation to the rest of the house. By running together from side to side we could make the carriage rock. All of this was done noisily, with wails and squeals and squabbles. Occasionally, we skipped out to find Mrs Lloyd holding her head in horror, her mouth ajar, eyes rolling back so far that we thought she might die. But she said nothing, relieved that we had once again survived the journey. She did not seem to be sure whether this new piece of machinery was designed for sport or terror.

Late one evening while my uncle was out, the lift stopped unexpectedly between floors. We were trapped. I clambered up the gate until my eyes were level with a slot of light on the next floor, and I called for help. We heard thundering up the stairs. Agnes and Mrs Lloyd appeared at eye level, on their knees.

"Make it go. Pull the lever," they shouted unhelpfully. "You cannot stop it there."

"It won't go. It is stuck," Fanny replied.

"Oh, my Lord. Oh, my Lord," Mrs Lloyd said, "I will get a broom."

Brooms fulfilled a thousand purposes in Mrs Lloyd's economy, but its usefulness at that moment eluded me. Agnes jammed her feet against the metal frame and her meagre body weight forced the gate ajar.

I scrambled down and unlatched the gate and it slid open. There was now a small crawl space to get out, if only we could reach it.

"Take hold of the broom and I will pull you out," Mrs Lloyd called.

"No, me first," Fanny screamed. "You are tall, Kate. If I get left behind who will push me up?"

"What about Jess?" Agnes asked.

"We can't get her out. She won't hold on to the broom," Fanny said.

Fanny climbed onto my shoulders, took hold of the broom, and with me pushing her legs, she was pulled swiftly through the gap, squealing all the way. Just as her feet disappeared, the elevator gave a shudder and jerked into motion. It creaked slowly back down to the ground floor, the gate still wide open, Jess perched perilously on the edge of the seat with me. My uncle, ashen, was standing staring into the void as we arrived.

"Did Fanny just climb out?" he demanded. "Between floors?"

I nodded cautiously. He was agitated. I steered Jess quietly past him. His hand locked around my arm, and he jerked me back to face him.

"I expect you to be more responsible for watching the girls," he bellowed.

"You're hurting me."

He released my arm. "Fanny could have been crushed to death."

"But I am not dead," Fanny declared, arriving at the bottom of the stairs flushed with excitement.

"You will be dead when I get hold of you," Angus said. "Take everyone upstairs out of my sight, please, Kate. That gave me the fright of my life."

I took Jess away and attended to her with unusual benevolence. We took refuge in the pretence of sleep until it was clear my uncle was not coming up to lecture or read or pray. Fanny sat up and sighed: "Was that not the most exciting adventure? We almost got caught."

"We got caught," I assured her. "That is why we are in bed."

"But I got trapped. I could have died. What a lark, Kate."

"I'm not doing it again," I said firmly. "Your papa was angry. He scared me."

"We scared him," she said triumphantly. "At least we are not getting the blame."

Sure enough, downstairs all the women in the house were being scolded by Angus. Aunty, who had slept through everything, was called down to lend support, although she could not imagine what the

3

The Teaching Assistant

James's bad-tempered vigilance over the classroom was harrowing, but it was mostly directed at Fanny. Although I knew he was rightfully disillusioned with life in general, I could not understand why he searched out all Fanny's little failings. It was equally hard to defend Fanny when she was lazy and rude. At times she was a willing scapegoat. James was surprisingly patient with the younger children, but they were my responsibility.

As the season changed and the days lengthened, light breezes lifted the dirty fog until the air was once again tolerable. I longed to be outside. Just being in the once beautiful parlour of Parmiter where my mother had presided over the silver service, made me remember everything I had lost. If a lump came into my throat, I shook myself firmly into the present moment, refusing self-pity. My childhood was vanishing, and the gulf between me and the other children was widening. James gave me Fanny's compositions to mark, and she was angry and confused when I tried to explain her errors. She unloaded her resentment on me at home. No one would agree with me that her mind was muddled. She could not organise herself, and everything dropped out of her memory. No words of mine – and none of James's barked instructions – resolved her difficulties.

It was probably because our friendship was slipping away, that I bargained for her continuing affection by sharing secrets. I brought out my precious bundles of letters that had fallen from the roof years earlier. We sat huddled over the letters that her mother, Helene Parmiter, had written to her half-sisters when they were away at school. I had to explain the details, because she did not know that Uncle Marriot had two wives, or how the Elliot, Marriot and Parmiter families were related. Fanny read the letters carefully, her forefinger following the sentences, pausing and rereading and crying. I had not expected tears. I put my arm around her.

"I'm sorry, I should not have given the letters to you."

"Papa has never told me anything at all about my mother," she said, mopping the tears with her sleeve.

"He does not like to dwell on the past," I said. "Don't be sad."

"No, I'm not sad. I'm happy to find out that I really did have a mother, and she was lovely," she said. "It just creates so many new problems for me."

"What problems?"

"I don't know who we are going to marry," she said.

I said indignantly: "Marry!"

"Yes. Don't you see? Your mother and my mother married their cousins. Where are our cousins? Your brother is dead. I could have married him."

"We don't have to marry cousins. My grandfather thinks it is bad eugenics for cousins to marry," I replied.

"Stupid man," she said, tears plopping down onto our mothers' fragile old letters as she surrendered to her inexplicable misery. "If we don't have cousins to marry, we will have to marry complete strangers. Can you imagine that? Papa has not planned this very well."

James had not planned our days well, either. By 11 o'clock every morning I craved some fresh air, the lavatory and a cup of tea. There was no relief to the monotony of the morning. James was not receptive to my suggestions that we have an interval to refresh our concentration. There was no play in Mr James's school, so my pupils began wriggling irritably in their seats, weariness creeping over them. Twice, little girls wet their knickers, and I had no spare clothes to resolve the embarrassment. Each time I complained to Aunty about our sedentary school day, she stopped knitting long enough to consider the problem and make new excuses for James.

"I suppose if James does not enjoy going for a walk, he probably does not consider the needs of more energetic folk," she said, smiling in her benevolent way.

"Kate's like a big puppy who needs exercising," Angus remarked. He had not been listening. "Do you want to go out for a long walk, so you can have a run?"

"Not me, Uncle Gus," I said firmly. "I'm very grateful that you exercise me like your big hairy dog, but I am referring to my pupils. They need to go out and play after ninety minutes of sitting. I need a cup of tea as well."

"Of course you do," he said firmly. "I teach in little bites. Much more effective than long hours of struggle. Perhaps you could write a report for James on what you have observed with your pupils. He likes having everything in writing."

"Very proper," Aunty said. "Include it in the curricula."

I spent a week carefully composing my report. Aunty helped me with newspaper reports and some of her old books on teaching, to prove my argument. When I presented it to James he skimmed through it with a peculiar smirk, his head tilted arrogantly.

"Do you think I am aspiring to run an elite girls' school?" he asked cynically. "Perhaps a little cricket?"

"They need fresh air and exercise every day for their health," I insisted. "We only need to go out to the field above the brook. Then they need a drink of water and an apple and the lavatory."

He tossed my notes aside: "Nature has fled. It is a rubbish dump out there."

"The field has been slashed and cleaned," I said.

Nort had reclaimed trees and bushes, patches of bulbs and wildflowers had reappeared, the orchard was flourishing, every tree was shored up with piles of manure carted from the streets. James's flippant dismissal annoyed me, because he had not seen Nort's handiwork, and he had no interest in what the old man did with his time.

"You took me exploring in that field when I was their age," I argued. "It was very educational."

He shrugged, stubbornly disinterested. I went back to my pupils. Ten minutes later he announced to the small group: "It is 11 o'clock. Miss Kate will now take you for a twenty-minute natural science excursion in the meadow."

I spun around and spat out my contempt: "Why are you so contrary?"

"Don't speak to me like a sullen child," he said. "I just thought about the pros and cons for a moment. I have never taught little children."

I gathered my charges and took Jess's hand and dashed towards the bridle path. In the swamp, the tadpoles were growing their legs, the little ringed plover had returned to nest, and we found the setts of nocturnal badgers. Fanny followed to the point where the path began to plunge down into dense green dampness, then she sat down on a flat stone. She could go no further. I gave the children a biology lesson.

"How do you know all this?" she called to me. "We are always together so I don't know how you find out things about birds and nests."

"Mr James showed me these things out here when I was small. I never forget anything once I learn it. I can hardly believe the badgers are still here, when there was so much rubbish dumped."

"I am so proud of you, Kate. You told off Mr James. You sounded so grown up."

"Don't say that in front of the children. I was not trying to be difficult," I said.

Despite James's turbulent nature, I was interested in the plans for my matriculation. He had challenging ideas, good topics for essays and research projects, and if we talked about the work, we managed to get along. Every afternoon he explained the books we needed to borrow from his father's library.

"You are ready to read Jowett's translation of Plato, Kate," James said. "Aunty says it was read at Cheltenham. If Aunty doesn't have time to work on your Latin we will have to push on with Greek, which is my stronger suit. You need a language for the King's Medal to get into a college when you are eighteen."

"You can't make her do all that," Fanny protested.

"I want to do it," I said, tapping my finger on my lips to hush her.

Once we got home Fanny went to bed, worn out by the school day, no matter how little she had achieved. Her sewing was always nearby, her embroideries growing by small increments daily, her darling cats purring and pregnant.

"Lay beside me Kate and read me a story," she pleaded. "Papa has bought me this new book called the Magic Garden."

"It's the Secret Garden," I said.

"It's got orphans in it," she said.

"I really don't need any more stories about orphans," I said, taking the book and sliding in beside her. "I'm living one of my own."

When she dozed off, I ached to go up the walnut tree that I was really too old to climb. From the tree top I could see clear across the meadow to the dark tenements. I wanted to wander to the trickle of dank water where the brook had once flowed, study the stones, pluck apart trumpet flowers and search the brambles for berries. I wanted to sit and listen to the distant drum of the streets, the late evening clanking and bellowing. I wanted to be alone. Everyone needed me. Pearl came running to me for help with trivialities. I was pursued by Agnes with questions about the washing. Mrs Lloyd wanted me to make up the shopping list. Angus was only satisfied if he heard me at the piano, or the violin. In the evenings, when he wanted to get the crick out of his hips, he liked to have me pounding along on the cobblestones at a great pace beside him, listening to reflections on what he had heard of my practice, or the examinations he would supervise in Manchester and Liverpool, his concerts, his troublesome sopranos, and his latest compositions. Helping Angus was more interesting than helping anyone else. Sometimes he wanted me at a rehearsal to conduct the choir while he was at the piano, or we changed roles, or I joined his chamber orchestra when musicians were missing. There were a thousand things to do in the studio, but I knew the reason for every task, particularly preserving the scores in working sets. I had relinquished page turning to Pearl, who was only good for a few bars before she lost concentration and missed the nod of my uncle's head. He would suddenly become impatient and snap, "Turn, Turn." At the slightest sign of an eruption Pearl leapt from the stool and fled in tears.

"Kaaaaaatyyyyyy..." my uncle bellowed up the stairs.

"I won't turn pages," I shouted back. "I'm busy."

"Kaaatyyyyy," Pearl howled, needing comfort.

"Give the girl some peace. She is a tinder box ready to ignite," Aunty chided.

"Ten minutes Kate and I will not trouble you again," Angus said. "You're such a dependable girl. Good lassie."

I dutifully did everything he asked because I prized his high opinion. I did not even shy away from giving respectability to his pursuit of ladies in public places. His latest, Gladys Drown, was his only diversion to escape the house, and I was, inevitably, summonsed as a quasi-chaperone. The hated houndstooth coat still hung on its sturdy wooden hanger behind the bedroom door. After my uncle had checked on Fanny taking her rest, he picked up the coat to tease me that it had cost a fortune to clean and needed its constitutional. I had grown another three inches, and the coat moved elegantly as I walked. Gladys admired it. A stout serious woman, she had green eyes and masses of auburn hair which she wore in a loose chignon. She walked a pair of fashionable little white dogs on the common, and by day she managed the Mare Street butchery, the first of a chain of thriving shops opened by her late husband. She was a Quaker, a pious woman who referred to the Good Lord as though he would appear momentarily. Her conversation interested me because I had conscientiously worked through the books and pamphlets James had supplied, with accounts of white slave trading, the emotional evangelicalism of Sankey and Moody, Whitefield and Wesley, the Corn Laws, the historical feminist roots of the suffrage movement, the Webbs, and the Irish potato famine. I was tending towards socialism, agnosticism and home rule. I imagined a Quaker church where everyone said nothing, would be a great relief.

With Gladys my uncle lacked his usual courtly manner, so that they were like an old married couple occupying the same section of a park bench, tossing ideas like a deflated football. I was not sure it was even a flirtation. Angus bestowed his real affection on her dogs. She was like a pretty, fading bisque doll, and she lacked the vivacity that Angus looked for.

"She doesn't hold a candle to Dr Stowe," I told him.

"Her character is strong," he replied dourly.

"But you won't marry her, will you?" I tormented.

"No, Kate, I canne marry any woman while I have a house full of naughty little lasses," he responded in his teasing tone.

When we arrived home late, Fanny was awake again, miserably hot, her back aching, her feet hurting, her eyes and head sore. All her frustration was stored up for me.

"Do not leave me alone for so long when I am ill," she rebuked me, "I do not want to die alone."

"You are not going to die," I said.

"I may die."

"You may not,"

We considered this idea solemnly for a few moments.

"If I was dying," she said, her eyes brimming with self-pity, "You should make sure I have a proper deathbed scene, with you and Papa, Aunty and everyone telling me how wonderful I am."

"I will arrange everything," I said.

"Don't you be ungrateful Kate Elliot," she said, her anger flaring when she recognised my cynicism. "What will happen to you if I am not here? Papa brought you home by mistake. You were the wrong girl."

"Ridiculous. Anyway, I asked him to bring me home here."

"I heard you were meant to be Mr James's cash cow," she said.

"I don't even know what that means, and neither do you," I snarled.

She shrugged: "Agnes said it. But it is true that your old cook lied to Papa about who you were."

"And I suppose you think she would tell Agnes all this rubbish?"

"No. It was Papa told me."

"Papa would never tell you such a thing, even if it was true."

"It might have been Agnes who told me, then, I forget."

"No one tells Agnes anything."

"Your old cook told all sorts. She should have been hanged as a baby farmer. All her orphans came from baby farming, including you."

4
Does Not Suffer Fools Gladly

When Aunty came down for breakfast on Saturday, I had already gathered a pile of books to return to my grandfather's library at Hampstead.

"I can't watch the girls today," I told her. "I've got to get back here in time for the choir."

She watched in alarm as I bolted down some breakfast, still on my feet. The problems of the parlour school had escalated, and now encroached on my entire life. I was nostalgic for the Morning Lane school, where I had walked out of the gates at three o'clock, and simply forgotten it. Today, our sacred Saturday, Marriot's carriage was waiting for me. I was trying to read a to-do list between gulps of tea. Aunty peered over my elbow at the long list of new books I needed to retrieve, deciphering James's spidery handwritten instructions to me. She sat down heavily and took out her knitting needles and began working away at a frantic speed as she waited for her toast, glancing at me, perplexed.

"She has a dreadful lot of work, here," she told Angus, the moment he came in.

"Aunty is right, Kate," Angus said. "You don't have time to collect books from Marriot every week when you have the choir and orchestra to work with."

"That is not what I meant," Aunty said. "It's Saturday, and all of us should have a free day. Music should not distract her from the real business of education. But poor Jimmy is demanding."

She had used a theatrical whisper, as though I was not there.

"Music is my education," I said firmly.

"It is indeed," Angus agreed triumphantly.

"I don't really mind getting the books," I insisted.

"Then I don't understand the problem," Angus said.

"James will scold me to death if I don't get this done," I said.

"It cannot be that bad, Kate," my uncle said. "I think you take James too seriously. He has a very dry wit, somewhat sly."

"He's not very funny when he is always complaining, whining and shouting," I said.

"Complaining, whining and shouting," Angus repeated softly. "Dear Lord, how harsh and critical you are. That poor man. I hope none of my pupils makes those accusations against me."

"Your character is not so difficult," I said. "At least, not in the same way."

Aunty nodded, and taking her peace maker tone, said: "You must understand that James does not suffer fools gladly. Whereas you, Gus ..."

There was a long silence. She had talked herself into a corner.

"Do I suffer fools?" Angus asked.

"You do," Aunty and I said in unison.

Aunty grinned at me, happy to agree. We were like a pair of contemptuous cats, adversarial yet never entirely hostile, able to reach a peaceful covenant. I could curl up next to her as she read to Fanny, safe in the knowledge that she loved us. Angus went out to make toast, and she spoke to me frankly: "James has a much stricter approach to teaching than Angus. Angus is far too lenient with everyone. I am sure that underneath it, James is very fond of you."

"I am sure he is not," I said indignantly.

"I feel like these two uncles are competing for your time. When do you get some time to yourself?"

"I don't," I said. "I have got too many jobs to do."

"It's good to have responsibilities, but just tell me what your biggest burden is at the moment."

"It's Fanny," I said. "She is not keeping up. She is losing ground. In fact, her brain seems to shut down. In some ways she used to be very clever, but now, nothing stays in her memory."

Auntie put down her knitting and nodded solemnly. "Are you saying that Fanny can't learn?"

"She just doesn't seem quite right in the head," I said. "Giving her detention when she is too tired to finish her work, is just cruel."

These fatal words fell out of my mouth and dangled in the silence. Aunty was alarmed, but she did not contradict me. Although it was Angus who needed to hear me, because he seemed flippant about Fanny's behaviour, I knew I could rely on Aunty to advocate for us.

"Uncle Gus blames me every time Fanny gets a detention, as though I can change the tide in the Thames," I said. "Mr James either wants me to stay back and supervise detention or come home and tell my uncle all about Fanny's dreadful behaviour. I have asked him to not make me his messenger."

Aunty was listening intently as I explained that fifteen minutes of detention was a crisis for Fanny. She needed to eat and sleep, rather than write 500 words on the economy of the Elizabethan age. Aunty nodded as I described how I felt guilty when they gathered around the afternoon teapot for me to explain Fanny's latest recalcitrance, and for them to discuss the injustice of this imposition on Fanny. She knew the scenario well. For Angus there was always a tight schedule because his studio classes began at four o'clock and continued until seven. He consulted his watch with irritation: "How much work has she yet to do?" he asked me.

"She is too tired to do anything," I responded. "And Mr James is ruthless."

"Ruthless? What kind of word is that?"

"Don't make Kate responsible for Fanny's behaviour," Aunty chided.

Rebuked and repentant he asked in a conciliatory way: "Can't you just explain to James how tired she is?"

"You are the father." I said.

"You are there all day."

"You are the adult. This was your idea. You have locked your daughter up with a hard task master and she is not able to do this work."

"Don't blame Angus," Aunty said. "I do not approve of detention at this time of the day. Girls in their maturing years do get tired. If James would just send her home with the work, I could help."

Right on cue, Fanny appeared at the door, red-eyed, drooping, her colourless face scrunched into knots of angry protest.

"I hate Mr James. I hate that school, and I want to go back to the one in Morning Lane," Fanny sobbed.

Angus pulled Fanny sympathetically to his side so that he could massage her temples.

"Overstrain of the nervous system," he said. "Uncle Marriot said it was a danger for girls."

"I think it's an old wives' tale," Aunty said huffily. "Old man's tale - against education for girls." She smiled at her own joke.

"I will speak to my cousin," Angus said, ignoring the barbs. He was on his feet, ready to go back to the studio schedule.

"Fanny needs another doctor," Aunty called after him, as she examined Fanny's misty eyes and pale complexion. "There are two sick people in that classroom,"

Angus paused momentarily but before he could retort, she added, "Your Dr Stowe, that dreadful woman, suggested we should find a doctor who can come every week, because this condition is chronic. A doctor such as my Dr Broadhurst. I might call him."

"Why is Dr Stowe a dreadful woman?" Pearl asked.

My uncle nodded agreement, no doubt relieved Aunty would take responsibility for the doctor. Pearl's question had been ignored until Mrs Lloyd stepped past to collect the cups. She glanced meaningfully at Aunty, who muttered: "She's back in a Boston marriage again."

Mrs Lloyd tutted loudly for several moments and asked: "Is she with one of those suffragettes?"

Aunty's eyebrows confirmed what Mrs Lloyd has surmised.

"They are like schoolgirls," Mrs Lloyd said.

Aunty's profile arched at the insinuation: "We did not allow such friendships at our school."

I searched the dictionary in vain for any reference to Boston marriages.

5
Truce

Aunty initiated peace negotiations, and Mr James came to Morning Lane for the reconciliation. To manoeuvre himself the short distance from his front door to ours was as complex as shifting an ocean liner in dry harbour. He arrived just on dark. He was on two new black sticks with brass heads and handles, and there was a bottle wrapped in newspaper protruding from a pocket of his coat. I had been concentrating on a composition at the practice organ when I saw the top of his head bobbing slowly past the studio window.

"Agnes," I called. "He's here. Fetch the professor. Bring drinks."

As I opened the door, I took the bottle from his pocket and asked in alarm, "What would have happened if you had fallen on broken glass?"

"Nasty," James said with a twisted little grin. I wondered if he had already been drinking because his voice was lilting and his mood light. He staggered along behind me back into the parlour.

"Is this why Pearl calls you the little mother, because you are so bossy?" he asked.

"Pearl told you that?" I asked, stunned.

"Little children tell all," he laughed.

"She has no mother, poor little girl," I said to deflect attention. "My uncle has been very remiss in providing any of us with a mother."

He laughed aloud. "Is that a joke?"

"No. We all want him to find a wife," I retorted.

"We all want one of those," he said. "Gus gets more opportunity than most of us."

I was startled by this intimate admission. The boundary lines had shifted. I wondered if Aunty's goodwill could have effected such a change in James. Perhaps she had already given him a good talking-to.

"I've sent for alcohol, and called for my uncle," I said.

He laughed aloud again: "Gus isn't the only uncle you have, you know, even if he is your preference."

I had the momentary satisfaction of thinking that James was offended by my affection for Angus. Then I saw he was amused. Perhaps this was what Angus regarded as James's dry and sly wit. There was clarity about his eyes, and a flush of youth in his cheeks. I felt awkward in this odd moment of intimacy, but when I began to move away, he held up his claw to stop me. He had something significant to say, and I was not sure I wanted to hear it. I waited while he squared me up, troubling his mind for the right phrases, his mouth twitching in its characteristic imitation of a small foraging animal.

"I am sure I do not need to explain why it was – why it is – impossible for me to do for you what Gus has so ably done?" he said, in sorrow. "I have limitations that, unfortunately, affect the guardianship. It was ridiculous for the relatives to imagine I can be an effective guardian."

"Uncle Gus will be glad you are here for a drink," I said, anxious to change the subject.

"Kate, I am so grateful to Gus for giving my life purpose," he said earnestly. "I really want this school to succeed. I am grateful for your help. I need your cooperation. That is all I am asking."

I was grateful for his restricted mobility, because it enabled me to escape his gaze. I had no answer for either his gratitude or his plea. Thankfully, Angus swept into the parlour, followed an instant later by Mrs Lloyd wheeling the tray of port wine, whisky and brandy, brandy balloons and small sturdy crystal cups, cheese under a dome and a pile of buttered crusts. I left as the two men clasped hands across the tops of the lead crystal decanters. To my dismay I saw the fresh warmth of their cousinhood. Much later I heard their voices amplified in the well of the lift, the clanking of the lever and the deafening whine of its mechanisms. Their laughter came in waves through the silence of the house.

I read late in the library, alone in the glow of the electric light, bemused by their play, until Aunty came in to ponder whether it was wise for two grown men to be cavorting in the lift after a drinking session. It was a long discussion.

In the morning, we were told about their agreement. When the small children finished their lessons and went home for dinner, to save time the older girls would eat a cold collation with Mr James in the scullery. Fanny was furious.

"I will not eat in that house," Fanny said. "I am going to come home with my sisters."

"Is that it?" I asked. "Three hours for that?"

"You will get home half an hour earlier," he said. "You will be here for your music pupils."

"What problem will that solve for Fanny?" I demanded angrily.

Angus turned to his aunt with his hands thrown out in despair: "I can no longer sort out biology from sheer bloody-mindedness. How long will it go on with these girls?"

"I need to point out that you and I, Gus, did make a priority of Fanny," Aunty said with studied calm, "This is not characteristic of female biology. Either Fanny is unwell and unreasonable, or you need to be firmer with her. There is a fine line of over familiarity that makes teaching impossible. Kate is not bloody-minded."

Angus scowled at me until he had my attention.

"But I think Kate is bloody-minded, Aunt. I think Kate makes the bullets that Fanny fires," he said.

I stood up: "Then I will fire a few bullets of my own," I said icily. "Since this school started, we can't keep nannies because there is not enough work for them to do. So now I am the teacher for Jess and Pearl all day at school and nanny all night at home. Fanny can't keep up with the work we are doing, and I must help her in the afternoon. I no longer have time for any dimension of my own education. This school is not working."

"It is working for you," Aunty said firmly. "If we took the other girls out of the equation, it would be a very fine school for you. Let's just solve the servant problem, Angus, and give Kate her time back properly."

School enrolments for the new term had fallen again, probably because James could not depend on his legs. We ignored his frequent falls. His housekeeper, Mrs Russell, responded swiftly to the dull thud and the jangle of his ornamented canes. Nort appeared silently to pick up the bundle of stick limbs, plonk him into the upright leather wingback chair, dust off his trousers and vanish again without thanks or comment. Mrs Russell brought tea and a nip. After these falls, a mother would withdraw her frightened child. Angus recruited a few more children, but their tenure was brief. There was uncertainty in the eyes of the mothers when they observed James's lurching gait.

Once the little children went home, James worked on classical languages, science, mathematics and ancient history. Three other girls who were preparing for matriculation joined these lessons, while Fanny worked alone on tasks to help her catch up. James was relaxed with us, and probably because he enjoyed the work, he was rarely terse. He introduced us to Mendeleev's Periodic Table of Elements, the configuration of the night sky, its stars and planets, the anatomy and physiology of species, and Mr Darwin's theories. We discussed, politely and objectively, genetics and eugenics, anthropology and geography, politics and economics, the principles and policies of universal suffrage, and designs for government. I learned to make reasoned oral defences of my opinions, and I began to accept his corrections and contradictions, as helpful. He taught us to look for the subtext in everything we read, the writer's unspoken prejudices, the hidden perspective, the persuasive impost of every adjective. With each new literary insight he shared, I saw more deeply into his world, but it was joyless and dark. So much of what he taught me had already been discussed at meals, although Angus offered only one dimension of Pythagoras – piano tuning – while James presented the sweep of the man's genius. The two uncles had opposing world views. Angus saw music as central to the renaissance and the restoration of civility, but James saw the chaos, murder and mayhem of ancient times as social evils that were just around the corner again. Although they shared dissenter ancestors, both accessed Marriot's library, and they had attended the same school, there had been a divergence, so that each seemed to understand the world through the lens of his own disposition. Disposition, I decided, was the moderating factor in making meaning of life. It was hard to consider their dispositions without thinking about my own. Aunty said I was graceless. I often followed Fanny's lead, and simply said whatever was on my mind. I was fighting an impulse to meet the goodwill of adults with hard-boiled contempt. I did not know where my pessimism and anger came from. I wanted better values but on principle I could not accept any that were being offered to me by Angus or Aunty. At times I wondered if they would lose patience with me, and my comfortable existence would come clattering down around me. Yet I also knew that simply because of their politics and religion, they were tolerant.

Despite Marriot's reputation for being miserly, he went to Covent Garden regularly to buy books that James said were essential for my classical education. Marriot was awed that education for girls had become so serious.

"Are you telling me the University of London will accept a girl?" he mused.

"They have for many years now," I said.

"It's not Oxford," he said. "But, good enough for a girl."

Marriot allied himself with the project to get me a higher education. He recited the words of Ibsen, Montesquieu and Swift who had spoken of a new kind of woman, advising me earnestly against the excesses of the women who were shouting, marching and starving themselves in London, for the sake of the vote. Education, he thought, was an essential prerequisite, for any woman who presumed the right to vote. This opinion sounded as though Aunty had talked him around to my cause, and hers. He probably read her letters, even if he rarely responded.

"The suffragette friends of my cousin Philomena Oroton are making enemies in high places," he said darkly. "I don't know why she mixes with them. My sister Caledonia gave it all up years ago. More can be achieved through process. Not protest."

When we talked about my future – and he also presumed I would teach - he suggested that I should work with the elite: "The poor are always with us. Don't waste your talents on them. Don't let Gus pull you in that direction."

I never mentioned that I was fully convinced that women must have the vote, although I would not make a fool of myself for the cause. My grandfather talked in waterfalls of history. He began to give me small tokens that illustrated subjects in which I was immersed. He had admired the old queen and so he gave me a silk handkerchief bought by his mother to mark the Queen's Jubilee, halfpenny coins minted during the great moments of her reign, and a limited-edition copy of Queen Victoria's *My Highland Journal*. When I was studying Africa, he gave me a signed limited edition of Farini's account of the lost city of the Kalahari and his exposition of the Pigmy and M'Kabba dwarfs. Farini had been an acrobat and a partner of my grandfather's theatrical friends Dick Warner and Manny Warner, names dredged up often, as though I might know them. He advised me to consult the fifth volume of English Historical Documents for 1485 relating to Henry VII's financial policy and Polydore Vergil's *Anglica Historia*. He piled up tombs for Nort to carry, insistent that there was no hurry for their return. Nevertheless, I always filled out his borrowing ledger with pride and signed my name with a flourish. I jiggled home happily to Hackney in a carriage left over from the dying age of the dear old queen. When

I arrived with my treasures, Fanny attacked me with resentment and contempt, until I felt robbed of all pleasure.

"You could have come with me," I said.

"I can't come with you. It's just about books. And I am not as energetic as you."

"You could just sit in the carriage."

"The old landlord is a murderer, like Mr James," she said.

"Oh please, Fanny, he is my grandfather. Don't make up stories about him."

"I heard Aunty telling the cook that he murdered Peter Parmiter and buried him under the floorboards," she said.

"Peter Parmiter drowned in the Serpentine, but they never found his body," I said.

"Or did he drown in the river under our house? Don't you think it's strange that everyone drowns in your family," she persisted.

"Oh grief, Fanny, that is so confused. Peter Parmiter is your grandfather. He's not my family at all."

This silenced her for a while. I waited for an inane response, but she whispered mysteriously: "You look so much like papa that people think he might be your real father. Remember someone said that?"

"Fanny, of course I remember. We have talked about this a hundred times."

"But you had a father, didn't you? Why do you like mine so much?"

"I didn't like my own father very much."

This seemed entirely reasonable to Fanny. She nodded and went back to her petit point. I was baffled by the meanderings of Fanny's mind. She lost the thread of the simplest conversations, no matter how many times we had trawled through the subject. Every night I tossed wakefully, wondering whether I was observing something malign, or simply Fanny's wild rebellious nature.

As we approached half term, tension increased in the parlour school because Fanny was too bored to listen and too tired to write or read. She kept falling asleep. James harassed her constantly. Unable to concentrate, her memory had become so vague that she was unresponsive to his simple questions. Fanny had been one of the best pupils at the Morning Lane school, but now she was slow. In the afternoon James just wanted to sit in his leather chair and expound from his notes. One afternoon as I watched with relief as the clock marched towards the close of the school day, Fanny began to pack up her books while James was still talking. He snapped at her coldly: "You have not even started your composition. You are not leaving here until it is mapped out."

Without warning Fanny screamed that she was going home. She slammed her books into a pile and marched towards the door. Guessing her intentions James hauled himself upright and splayed himself across her path like a tin soldier: "Sit down and be quiet," he roared.

I lowered my head further into my own work. My stomach churned in protest as the simmering hostilities between them cracked open the quiet afternoon. James nodded to the other girls in the room, and they packed up and scurried away, glancing over their shoulders in curiosity and fear. He continued to block Fanny's escape.

"Get out my way. I could push you over, you know," Fanny shouted contemptuously. "I could make you fall on your face." As her destructive threats resounded shockingly around the empty room, I realised that the parlour school had no recognisable boundaries for Fanny. It was too ambiguous, without a real classroom of children, with me as a teaching assistant and Poor Jimmy as the master, and all of us locked up in a single room for the day. For Fanny, no one had any authority, and she felt no obligation to show respect. I felt the futility of what I was doing here. I just wanted to escape, even if it meant cricket and hockey and Scottish reels in a faraway school for girls. I needed to go off to Cheltenham and have space and time again, and not be the little mother to a colony of children.

"Kate hates you," Fanny snarled. "Don't think she likes you, just because she is polite."

"Control your tongue," he said. "Do not say anything you will regret."

"Here is something you will regret," she said. Her voice was low and hateful: "Kate said you killed her brother. That's why she hates you. My father hates you, too, because you are going to steal our house. We will be out on the streets because of you."

Her accusations were more malicious than anything I had heard before. They were taunts intended to destroy the fragile thread of goodwill we had created in the classroom. The fantastic stories I had spun about Cyril, had been regurgitated as fact. I should have known this would happen. Yet Fanny's pronouncement about 55 Morning Lane was entirely new. I could not imagine who gave her that information. She was no longer capable of making up stories.

I lifted my eyes cautiously from my work to see Fanny's head wobbling, her eyes unfocused, beads of sweat pouring down her sallow cheeks, her chest heaving. It was as though she had left her own body. It occurred to me that Fanny had been sprouting some kind of madness, and like a rabid dog, she was no longer in charge of herself.

"Please let Fanny go home," I pleaded with James urgently. "There is something wrong with her. I could run down and get my uncle to carry her home."

"She is out of control, that is what is wrong," he said.

"She is not normally so out of control. This is not normal," I said.

"It seems perfectly normal to me. She has been behaving wretchedly from the first moment I clapped eyes upon her. I was a fool to imagine I could modify a girl as undisciplined as this one."

James leaned against the door, determined we would not leave. Fanny's arms were stiff and trembling, her hands shaking uncontrollably, her head arched back, reddening with rage, a tiny, suppressed scream emitted through her clamped mouth. I wanted to slap her until she stopped, but I did not move, certain that this was another manifestation of her condition. Then she crumpled to the floor, her entire body vibrating so hard that she was moving across the room, veins protruding, her neck thrust forward.

"Fanny, please stop," I said. I knelt beside her. This was not a faint. Perspiration was pooling around her neck. She gulped air, her eyes open, fixed on me, unseeing. Slowly I pulled her to her feet and moved her back to the desk, and she put her head down on her arms and immediately began snoring in a deep sleep. James opened the door and called out wearily to the housekeeper: "Can you walk down and see if Professor Elliot will come and take Fanny. She has made herself poorly."

He turned back to me and said: "Angus might come and explain to me whether this is biology or bloody-mindedness."

The familiarity of the words alarmed me. I remembered the words from a tea-time conversation between Angus and Aunty, and I felt trapped in the double standards of adult loyalties. There was no one I could trust.

"This is hysteria," James said. "No man can tolerate this nonsense. I have had enough of it."

"She has not been like this before. She is not responsible for anything she said."

"No. You have been making the bullets," he snapped.

His accusatory words were another echo of words spoken by Angus so recently at Morning Lane. Now I had two uncles colluding to condemn me. I hovered over Fanny, unable to focus on my own tumultuous emotions when she seemed broken. Eventually, her breathing steadied and her body relaxed. Sensing the crisis has passed, James abandoned his guard on the door. He slipped the leather rest of his new crutch under his armpit, scuffing across the room to where I had been working at his standing desk, parsing the remarkably apt words of the Greek in the Gospel of John 2:5 *Whatsoever he saith unto you, do it.*

"I do not care if you do not like me," he said in a harsh whisper as he checked my work. "I did hope for a little gratitude and respect. But I was not expecting this nonsense from you. Did you think you were entitled to this house or some other property?"

"I have no idea what Fanny was talking about. I have never thought about who is entitled to this house," I said.

"You go to my father's place often enough. He only ever talks about real estate and his will."

"Not to me."

"Surely, he told you that he is transferring all the property to me, mostly slums and music halls, to avoid death duties, if he can live another seven years. Morning Lane is just another lease we own. Not my choice. Nothing I ever planned or anticipated. Not something I covet."

"He did not tell me," I said. "I don't even understand what it all means."

"Wait here until Gus comes."

I packed up my copy book, bible and pen, but I could not hold my peace.

"I want to speak to you," I called after him.

"What now Kate? Have I not been persecuted enough for one day?"

I went out into the hallway and saw he was coatless and shivering, hair dishevelled, his tie loose and collar open. He had just ripped off his jacket and thrown it on the floor. When I began to speak, my tone was confessional: "I did not say exactly what Fanny thought I said. I just made-up stories about my brother. It was not serious. Just joking."

"What a bizarre and disgusting topic for jokes and stories," he said. "Your brother's death, a source of amusement? Obviously, you hardly knew him."

The truth slapped at my senses. I searched for words to restore my reputation or make peace. I found a stronger voice when I spoke again: "I did not know Cyril. The only person who talked about him was my grandfather. I did not know anything about his death until my grandfather told me that you dived into that river at Colden Bridge and tried to rescue Cyril, and now your legs are bad from the cold water."

His murky eyes stared back at me, narrowing to slits of disdain with each word I spoke: "Did you believe that nonsense?" he demanded.

"Of course, I believe my grandfather."

He shook his head, his eyes alive with contempt: "My father always has some heroic myth for every tragedy. All my brothers died as heroes, you know. My father doesn't know what happened at that school," he said. "I cannot swim. I cannot dive. I could not rescue anyone. And as for my legs, no cold river was needed for this. It's in my family. Eugenics."

Before I could rein in my smouldering scepticism I sneered: "More secrets and lies, then?"

"My family is big on secrets," he said, matching my tone.

"I lost my whole family," I said, my throat taut with emotion. I was past caring about his opinion of me. "I have hated being here in this house. Every day I remember that my brother drowned, and you were there. You have never spoken a word about it. No explanation."

"What did you expect from me? I also lost all the real family I had at Colden Bridge," he said. "And now I live alone in their house, and by God, every day I wish I did not."

He was echoing my feelings about Parmiter. He portrayed himself as just like me. I struggled with the riot of resentment.

"I just need the truth." I said, sorrowfully.

His response was fierce: "Truth? Is that what you want? If all this turmoil and conflict ever since I arrived has been about Colden Bridge, then you deserve the truth." He paused for a beat, his dark eyes piercing me: "Cyril threw himself into the river at the lashers where there was no hope of rescue. He could not swim, either. I had to identify his body when it was pulled out miles downstream. I loved him like a brother. I lived in this house like your brother when I was a young man. Oh yes, and I had to subscribe to the lies that were told by the school for fear of what they might suffer for the way the boys hounded Cyril to his death. Because he was not like them. Bullies. School bullies, Kate. Cruel, careless, unkind, tormenting bully boys, behaving just like you and Fanny."

His condemnation burst into my conscience. His explanation made sense. I had seen the terrifying torrent of the river when I was ten years old, and it was inconceivable that anyone would take a skiff into those waters. Surely, to enter those waters was a reckless and desperate act. Surely nothing we had done could lead anyone to such despair. I now had a glimpse of the grief that suffocated my parents in the last five years of their lives. It was not a simple accident. Had they known that their only son threw away his life? Or was it the deception and a senseless lie that tormented them? I needed to run and breathe clean air and escape the venom that had come out of James's mouth. I could not believe that boys, my age, could hound another child to his death. James's accusations were a crucible.

I turned to leave, and James roared once more: "Stay here, I have not finished telling you the truth. The boys at Colden Bridge made a mockery of private matters. I lost my living. I lost my reputation. And then I come here to have you make a mockery of those same matters."

"You are cruel to Fanny," I said. "You have bullied her. She is sick."

"We started this school for your benefit. I honoured your place in this family as though you were your father's daughter."

"What are you saying?" I demanded. "Are you saying I am not my father's daughter? That is a lie."

"I was told that by your father. It is common knowledge. That is why it made no sense when my father harassed me to come back to England and take responsibility for you. And here I am, now. Honouring the lie. Putting up with this abuse from you."

"You're a liar," I shouted. "That's the kind of lie that has been going around this family for years. Shouldn't I be the one to know if it was the truth? You are a liar."

Two hands landed hard on my shoulders. It was Angus, his face dark, voice barely audible: "Go home, Kate. I don't know what is happening here, but I think you've said enough."

I shook myself free and shrieked: "Go and see what he has done to your daughter."

"Go home," he repeated. I shrugged off his hands and as I turned to run, I heard him say gently: "Oh Jimmy I am so sorry. I cannot believe the trouble the girls are causing you."

6
Hallebloodydoodle

Fanny was limp when Angus hauled her up to his shoulder to carry her home from the parlour school. He had only taken fifty paces when, for the second time that day, Fanny's violent shaking began. Her legs jerked wildly, her eyes rolled back and vanished into a field of fine veins etched on a yellow sea. Then her limbs stiffened and trembled. Angus was pale and perspiring when he stumbled into the atrium and laid Fanny on a mat. He shrieked in panic: "Aunty. Aunty. Come quickly."

I went into the atrium cautiously, guiltily. He was haggard, like a haunted man, watching helplessly as Fanny's body vibrated into impossible contractions. When I realised that Angus was overwhelmed, I felt as though I would collapse. I put a hand against the wall to steady myself. Fanny's limbs began flailing again in a macabre dance, but she was not aware of anything. Angus had a hand under her neck, the other hand trying to still her, but she arched back on rigid muscles, her spine barely in contact with the ground. Involuntary movements were propelling her across the room.

Aunty ran down the stairs, her voluminous petticoats hitched up, and she dropped onto her swollen knees at Fanny's side. Her varicose veins bulged beneath her stockings. Without hesitation she used the hem if her frock to wipe a cloud of foam and mucus from Fanny's mouth and nose, pushed a handkerchief between the clenched teeth. She looked up at Angus reassuringly, "She is fitting. I have seen this before. It will pass in a few minutes. It will pass."

Fanny's jolting body travelled a full circle. Aunty shuffled after her on her knees, her skirts riding further up the soft rolls of wrinkled flesh on her thighs. It was an eternal moment, then Fanny became limp and her back dropped to the mat. Her eyes fluttered, and her head fell into her father's hands. It took me a full minute to realise she was sleeping, and not dead. Angus lifted her onto the couch under the stairs and the doctor was called.

Stunned and frightened, meals forgotten, I took Jess and Pearl up to my bed and played with them and read to them until they fell asleep. Aunty came up with their night gowns, but Angus would not let them be disturbed. He tucked them in to the single bed and recited the Lord's prayer over their soft snores, Aunty echoing his words. They bent down stiffly to kiss the girls' foreheads, and left, silent and solemn. I felt they had ignored me.

I went to a spare bed where I could be alone and recall the horrors of the day. Sleep evaded me. The spectre of Fanny fitting on the atrium floor troubled me. James's words troubled me. Who was I, and why did this accusation follow me? Not my father's daughter. What more did James know? The night passed slowly. I constantly examined the delicate gold watch on my wrist that Aunty had given me for my academic triumph at the Morning Lane school. I stroked its gentle contours, comforted by its presence. Angus had advised us to get the phosphorescent clockface that was visible at night. Fanny was delighted with the purchase, although she thought I needed a new coat more urgently. The days of jealousy and threats were gone. She depended on me, and her affection was genuine. As the night wore on, I tormented myself with resentment of Angus's clumsy fathering. Surely, he could not continue to ignore Fanny's devastating symptoms and deny the reality of her decline? She had stopped growing physically. She was not maturing emotionally. Then I played with fear of retribution for the war in the parlour school. I told myself that I had allowed Fanny to pull me into her vortex, so that her faults were mine, and I shared guilt for bullying Mr James. Was it even possible for two girls to bully a grown man? Yet how could I expect Angus to tolerate me when he was taking Mr James's side? How long before Aunty lost patience? I had no condition, my health was vigorous, I had no excuse. How could I justify myself? I was afraid Angus would want an explanation of my behaviour in the morning. Yet perhaps now, finally, Fanny's condition eclipsed everything. What was a fit? Why was is happening? I was restless with fury and grief. My heart felt broken, I had an open wound in my chest, and everything was falling out. Worse still, I was alone with my wound, without Fanny's sympathy. No one was interested in my pain, and anyway, I felt undeserving. I could easily relinquish centre stage to Fanny because I sensed this was her last act.

Discernment came with the dawn. I dismissed my last doubts and jettisoned my desperate optimism that Fanny was malingering. She was not feigning this macabre event. James had been stubbornly wrong in his assessment of the horror we witnessed in the school room. Her condition was extracting its full penalty. Angus was wrong in his inertia and optimism. Even Aunty had not applied enough pressure to make Angus realise the seriousness of Fanny's condition. I got out of bed and dressed, ready to go to war on Fanny's behalf. It was not needed. Angus and Aunty had not slept. They were sitting together at the breakfast table, overwhelmed and exhausted. Just as I entered the room, I heard Angus whisper: "I've been a fool. I just refused to see that this day was coming."

"We have to live in the good days God sends," Aunty said, her hand resting on his arm. "No parent wants to face the loss of a child."

They been like this making fresh tea and toast all night, fearfully alert in case Fanny had another crisis, anxious for daylight. They had sent out urgent calls for medical help, and it came as I waited with them. Dr Broadhurst led the way, followed by several colleagues. They looked like a flock of wild geese coming up the steep front steps. Their coats flapped open in unison in a bluster of wind. In the downstairs space under the stairs, Fanny was left alone with the doctors for almost an hour. I was sent back up the stairs to keep the other girls quiet.

Aunty was called on by the doctors first. Then the doctors were shut up for an hour with my uncle in his studio. When the doctors finally left, Angus invited James for tea, and they spent so long together that more crumpets were sent in to sustain them. The next day people paraded in and out of whispered conversations continuously. The daily help was taken into my uncle's confidence, and even the exiles, Miss Po and Dr Stowe, returned together and spent an hour in the parlour with Aunty and Angus. The women who were usually so stoic, emerged red eyed and alarmed.

It was evening before Angus assured me that the doctors were optimistic that the new treatment would help Fanny.

"I think you know where we are up to with this disease," he said, his hand brushing back my unkempt hair.

It was all I expected from him. It was not the moment to tell him about my broken heart. I wanted to say that I had been thrown under a steamroller, and no one had noticed. There was no moment for my pain. He said nothing about James. The problems of the parlour school were lost in the long shadow of Fanny's prognosis. I let relief and resentment continue to simmer together, silently.

A few days later, when Fanny regained some strength, she was forthright and informative.

"I have diabetes," she announced, almost proudly, as though it was her latest excuse for dissembling. "It's not just my horrible heart. Now there is something wrong with my kidneys. I didn't even know people had kidneys. I will never eat steak and kidney pudding again."

"Fanny, is this the truth?"

"Hallebloodydoodle," she said. I repeated the word thoughtfully. It was an oath used sparingly.

"All my life I knew I would die young," she said, with the same enthusiasm she had for embroidery patterns. "I am actually quite excited about going to heaven."

"Fanny," I gasped, appalled. "Do you really believe there is a heaven?"

"I do and you must, Kate," she said. "Of course it's true. Papa and Aunty said so too. It's not just the hallelujah girls who talk about heaven. It's in the bible."

"I know that. But the doctor is going to make you well again," I insisted.

"I will be so cross if the new powders don't stop me from being tired. They taste so bad. Anyway, I only want to finish my tapestries for the dining room chairs before I go."

"Before you go," I repeated, unbelieving.

Her index finger poked upwards. It was such a small ambition. All of life's wonderful possibilities were bypassed with her little expectations. I climbed into her bed, and we entwined. She tucked her head under my chin. Fanny had no memory of our last afternoon in Mr James's school, and I refused to enlighten her, particularly as the one thing she was most interested in hearing, was too dreadful for me to speak about.

"Did you see me having a fit?" she asked.

"Hallebloodydoodle," I said.

"Tell me, Kate. What happened? It terrified everyone. I can't remember anything."

Before I could speak, she fell asleep again.

I did not return to school that week, pleading sick headaches. Music became my refuge. I found complex new pieces to conquer, playing until my fingers knew their own way. My wrists ached and my fingers left a trail of blood across the ivories. One afternoon my uncle came in just as I was packing up, and he rested his hand on my shoulder, as though he wanted to talk. I expected encouragement from him. The school was not on my mind. So, I was shaken when he was direct and harsh: "You must make peace with James. Just forgive him and let it go. Go back to school and take the little girls. Your hostility is making everything so much harder than it needs to be. Go and apologise to James."

I wriggled away from him, "What? Are you telling me that I am the one who must apologise?" I asked indignantly.

"You cannot avoid him and avoid school. Just go there and sort it out."

"Do you know what he said to me?"

"I think it was a misunderstanding. It is just not important now," he said.

"It was important to me," I protested. "He trampled all over my life."

"James did not know what was happening with Fanny. He is sorry. We need James on our side. Especially now when properties are being sorted out."

"Properties? What properties? What is all this about properties?" I had raised my voice, and he raised an eyebrow. I did not lower my voice when I complained: "Fanny was saying something to James about properties, but you have told me nothing."

"I want you to be provided for in your grandfather's will, that's all. You have a right and Fanny does not. Perhaps that is what Fanny overheard and got upset about. I just need to keep a roof over all our heads when Marriot sorts out his estate."

"My grandfather would never take Morning Lane away from us," I said.

"It is still his property, not mine," Angus murmured. "I am a nephew and not a son. I have no right to anything."

"I don't care about properties or wills. I just don't want to go back to James's school," I said. "I will go to Cheltenham Ladies College. That was what Aunty suggested. I could start next term."

"It is no longer quite so easy, Kate," he said. "It is all out of my hands, now that James is home. He is your guardian, and he controls the purse strings, which is why you must keep the peace with him."

"No. After all this time you cannot let him just walk in and change my life. You should tell him what I want. What about my grandfather? I will ask him. He will pay for me."

"No Kate. Marriot is passing his financial responsibilities to James. You can't even think about Cheltenham unless you are on good terms with James.

If you apologise to James and go back to school, then we can all discuss the future."

"I can't believe that you let him boss me," I protested loudly.

"It sounds like you're bossing me," Angus replied in deliberate sotto voce.

I lowered my voice again. "James said dreadful things to me. You cannot imagine how angry I am."

"Yes, I can," he said. "I can hear your anger coming out of the piano every afternoon. Everything you play sounds like you are marching to war."

"Perhaps I have a right to be angry with all your secrets and lies."

"I have never lied to you," he said, offended. "Today I just want you to do as I ask. Go and make peace with James."

He kissed my forehead and left the room. I wanted to scream.

Fanny resumed the role of invalid with enthusiasm. She became everyone's project. Visitors trooped in and out, but none were as welcome as Dr Stowe who brought ribbons, bows, lace collars and tartan turndowns for socks. Twice Dr Stowe walked out with Angus, and she stayed late to sing with the Bach choir, and she came to rehearsals for the St Matthew Passion. There was an occasional spark when their hands touched accidentally, but no real romance was evident. Twice I heard their voices raised in the hallway late at night in anxious debates about Fanny. Then Dr Stowe was gone again. In her place came Mary Rycraft, one of the singing suffragettes. She fluttered around my uncle in a childlike way, holding his eye longer than he liked.

"Take Mary up to see Fanny, please," my uncle said, his tone a desperate appeal to escape her simpering attention. On some occasions Mary appeared without warning at the door of the bedroom, carrying a basket of fruit for Fanny, willing to read, do crossword puzzles and gossip. People imposed themselves on us, mentioning Fanny's condition as though it had become a volume in a public library. Even Miss Po made the journey upstairs with medicines and reading material, but she firmly refused to discuss Fanny's plea that I be bought a red coat. There was ten years wear left in the houndstooth, Miss Po said with satisfaction.

"It's my dying wish that Kate gets a new coat," Fanny said indignantly. Fanny found this phrase useful on many occasions. Her other dying wishes were, firstly, that Nort should find kind homes for a newly discovered litter of ten ginger kittens in the shed. Secondly, she wanted to win the final volumes of *Elsie Dinsmore* from the East End gospel mission. As much as I loathed Fanny's novellas, she craved the books.

"Elsie Dinsmore is so lovely even if she is only in a book," she said.

"Why don't you try something new?" I asked. "More grown up."

"Sometimes, Katy, I don't want to think about real life at all. I just like to curl up inside someone else's story so I'm not here anymore, being sick."

Her voice was heavy with a rare reflection on her own condition. showing me the depth of her pain. I resolved to always read to her, until she escaped into sleep. I would always ensure she had books to help her endure our own story.

Catching a bus to the mission was impossible for Fanny, so I tried to persuade Nort to take us on his cart. He explained with deep seriousness that the horse kept the Sabbath. Moreover, the horse came from the North and did not know its way home if he fell asleep at the reins. That stretched credibility, although Angus insisted it was true. In another torturous conversation with Nort, I asked about the fate of some more ginger kittens that he had scooped out of a gap in the wall behind the nursery. Smiling, Nort pointed through the window to all the good homes he had found - the red double brick outhouse that contained a pit lavatory at Parmiter.

Convinced that every adult in our household was descending into madness, I went alone to the mission just to win the last of the books for Fanny, by reciting scripture. I reasoned this was fair, because Fanny had learned scripture thoroughly, and she even believed it. We had recited swathes of it for our confirmation classes with Mr Robart, and Aunty ensured we memorised the whole of John's Gospel, emulating a teaching practice of the beloved Miss Beale, whom, she said, was also a true believer. I caught the tram alone, wearing a navy-blue beret and its companion coat, which had faded two shades lighter. Aunty had given both items to me. The coat had fitted her beautifully when she was 42, she said, but it had probably shrunk in the rain. It swamped me, but at least I was not a spectacle in the houndstooth.

At the door of the mission hall the little women in bonnets did not recognise me because I had grown into an even taller version of myself. I told them about Fanny's sickness. When I explained my plan to earn the Elsie Dinsmore books in Fanny's stead, they took me into the storeroom to select the ones she wanted. They were lovely, illustrated books with solid red and green covers glittering with gold type faces and improbable portraits of cherubic young females. The women also promised to pray for Fanny, which I assured them was not necessary because Angus was able to say perfectly good prayers. I was so embarrassed to receive the books without effort, that I impulsively invited them to visit. That afternoon they made a pilgrimage to Morning Lane. After all, they said, she was their convert. It was the first of too many regular visits. Angus was reliably courteous to strangers, but he was not happy to have gospel girls under his roof. They represented an invasive American religion that he did not trust. I pointed out that the Salvation Army came out of the North of England, but he was unimpressed,

"What were you thinking, Kate? They want to save her soul and have me sign the pledge etcetera. They are like vultures when anyone is ill. They are out to make proselytes. Converts."

"Too late," I said. "Fanny has converted. She believes she is going to heaven."

Angus protested, "Of course she is. But she could get there drinking whisky and without the brass band, if she read her bible properly."

I was baffled by my uncle's ambiguous religion, rejecting the temperance movement and yet embracing mystical notions of a heaven. Aunty was mortified by the gospel girls' zealous invocation of matters she considered too private for discussion. They asked her bluntly about the state of her soul, and she silenced them with rhetoric. Both Aunty and Angus soon overcame their prejudices for Fanny's sake. Each time the gospel girls came with new religious novellas, they left a deposit of hope that made Fanny optimistic for days.

"I am so proud of you, Kate. I can get free books now."

"But you do not even want to read them. I must."

"But free," she insisted.

"It is such puerile drivel," I said.

"Yes, but Elsie Dinsmore is so lovely."

I climbed into her bed to read to her, and we sat tangled in each other's arms. I loved her passionately, painfully, but she was not going to grow up. Her losses carved a claim on my conscience. I was captive to her whims, torn between pity for Fanny and anger at every adult who had pronounced her fate. Fanny, for her part, was my comforter. When she was strong enough to sit up to work on her petit point, she had romantic fantasies about my life, what I might do, where I might go, and the audiences that would adore me. I would be wearing a Lincoln green taffeta floor-sweeper to play virtuoso at King's Hall.

Fanny was meant to return to school for a couple of hours each day, but James was unwell and closed school until after half term. He appeared, quite well, to participate in the continuing drama at Morning Lane. I presumed he was doing penance when he sat in the bedside armchair, reading history to Fanny. She sent the cats out the window when he came, because they made him sneeze. It was the first time any person had been given preference over the cats. Pearl was waiting outside the studio to inform me, uneasily, that James was in my bedroom. She was now competently speaking in capitals so large that they deserved to be historiated. Moreover, she could supply gossip, because she had a remarkable interest in domestic politics. She had a lilting voice that she accented with gasps and exclamation marks.

"He has the key to the elevator, and he won't take me in it," she complained.

"It is Aunty's elevator," I said. "She can decide."

"Ezept she hates it," Pearl said with dark menace clouding her angelic eyes.

"Does Fanny want him in the bedroom?" I asked.

"Oh yes. She is allowed adult company, you know. Not me though. I am not allowed because I am a squealer. They play cards for pennies. Fanny wins."

"I think you like him," I said, glowering at her suspiciously.

She smiled at me shyly, nodding. I had noticed the strong affection spring up between them. Even if James was strident, she just hunched her shoulders and giggled. Fanny's tolerance of his company was more baffling. Her resentment vanished the moment they began playing cards together. I went up and peered through the crack of our bedroom door and saw James cosily ensconced in the watcher's chair, reading aloud. His voice danced lightly over the words of the history primer that Fanny had flung across the parlour of Parmiter months earlier. He paused, posed a question, and accepted her quiet answers with unusual tolerance. Fanny, in her weakness and vulnerability, had finally captured and tamed him. The anguish I felt when I saw Fanny laughing flirtatiously, was physical pain. Reclining contentedly on her pile of pillows, surrounded by her sewing and juvenile religious tracts, she had changed allegiance. I was alone in my indignant opposition to James. I had not apologised, and I avoided contact with him. However, when I was spying through the door, he sensed my presence and without turning, he called out my name.

"Kate. I have left some notes for you on the dresser downstairs," he said. "We will work on those topics as soon as school resumes."

I said nothing and ran to Aunty for sympathy. She spent the afternoons in a deep chair, books in her lap, studying Latin grammar in the thread of sunlight that came through the breakfast room windows, her large teacup steaming. She was rarely alone for long, because she listened to everyone in a way that I now recognised as essentially female, concerned with detail, retaining and recalling the continuity of our stories, asking pertinent questions, clarifying minor points. When she contradicted me there was no malice in it, and she rarely offered easy solutions. More importantly, she was confidential. When I sat down, she picked up her knitting, which seemed to require no concentration.

"Mr James is in my bedroom?" I said. "That can't be right. Where am I supposed to go?"

She looked up and smiled, "He is just visiting Fanny, like everyone else."

"Fanny doesn't want him there."

"Choose your battles carefully," she said. "Fanny loves him."

"He is not her family."

"Family is anything you want it to be," she said. "It may be time for you to move into another room. That room is not big enough for an invalid. It will always be full of visitors and doctors from now on. You need some privacy."

We sat in silence until I said: "I cannot understand why my parents would make James my guardian, after what happened with my brother."

"Kate, oh Kate, no," she said, and dropped her work into her lap and looked up in alarm. "Is this at the bottom of all this trouble with James? Are you blaming him for what happened at Colden Bridge?"

"He was supposed to take care of my brother at that school. If my brother had not drowned, my parents would never have gone anywhere near that river. He knows what happened. Do you know what happened? I can't forgive him."

It seemed she would not reply. I waited, expecting some sympathy, but she had none for me. She was shaking her head slowly.

"I don't want to know what happened," she said. "It changes nothing. It is a tragedy too great to revisit."

I stood up abruptly, ready to leave.

"Kate," she said. "Don't rehearse your wounded spirit."

"I don't know what that means," I said. "I am just saying I cannot forgive him, and I do not want to be near him. I don't want him in this house and especially not in the room where I sleep."

"He can't forgive himself," she said firmly. "His own father can't forgive him. From what Angus has told me, your parents could not forgive him. The man has been consumed by guilt for years. And now you won't forgive him either? How cruel. Kate, for all our sakes, forgive him, and do not make James your enemy."

"In case he takes our house?" I asked. "In case he doesn't give me my money?"

"In case you allow all your terrible losses to turn you into a dreadful shrew who lives in the past. I have sisters who analyse the Boer War, turning over every detail every day, to find someone to blame for their lost boys. We are given these trials in life to become a better version of ourselves. The more you rehearse your resentment, the bigger it will get. It will consume your life."

Before I had an opportunity to consider moving out of the bedroom, Fanny told me to go. She did not want me there anymore. I wanted to escape the smell of cats and the constant visitors and nights of broken sleep, but I shrank from the finality of going into a room alone. Agnes was surprisingly sympathetic. She helped me clean out the box room, and Nort brought in a suffragette bed and some beautiful, embroidered linens that had been found in a camphor box. Doubtless my mother's stuff pilfered by the old housekeeper. Aunty gave me money to take the bus to a departmental shop and buy a new feather down quilt. When the room was ready, I slept deeply, gratefully alone for the first time in years. It was the sleep of both relief and sadness, because I was no longer responsible for Fanny's deteriorating condition.

Fanny had relinquished me so callously, that I was surprised the next day to discover there were conditions for our separation.

"You must come back and read to me when I am ready to sleep," she instructed me.

When it was time to sleep, Fanny could not. She wanted to talk about those things we had not yet done. We had not danced or kissed boys, we had not had a social debut in taffeta and lace, with its opportunity to be dangled romantically by young men, and we had not worn shimmering gowns and gone out in the dark to glamorous places. Fanny's daydreams were anathema to her father. In realistic moments she conceded that our lot was probably to marry one of the boys who flocked around Angus. We would only improve ourselves by moving to Walthamstow with a shrubbery front and back, iris between the paving stones and some net curtains.

When sleep overwhelmed her, I remained in the chair, wrapped in the blanket, unwilling to go up to the unfamiliar room, turning over Aunty's words, wondering how anyone could be a better person in the midst troubles like this. Angus came in late to check on Fanny and the cats lifted their eyes and purred as he rolled his knuckles over their heads. They arched and stretched towards him, turned a half circle and settled peacefully back into the same dip in the quilt.

"Why don't we get tickets for a concert?" he suggested.

"Not now, Uncle Gus. I don't want nights out. I just want to be with Fanny."

"What would you like to hear?"

"I want to hear Elgar, but he's Roman Catholic."

He sighed: "I will find out where he is performing."

He wanted to kiss me goodnight, but when I shrank away from him, he left briskly.

I brooded over the injustice of Fanny's life and the lingering illness which made me cling to her. I often wished it was over. Whenever I realised her world had shrivelled to a space where she fit comfortably, I went down to the studio and revisited pieces we had learned together years earlier. Angus came into the studio and sat with his eyes closed. Sometimes he went to the other piano and we drifted into duets. At times I improvised, and he followed me. He enjoyed my creativity and laughed when I reminded him of his rule against noodling on the piano. Sometimes he offered musicology or plans for my future as a distraction from our crisis.

"If I took you to Brussels, you might be able to meet the conductor Ysaye," he said, mildly enthused. "They call him the king of the violin. He started out in a beer house band that became Berlin Philharmonic. If he heard you play, he might just take a girl of your age, for the summer."

"Fanny is so poorly. I need to be here for her."

"Fanny is drawing away from us," he said. "I want you to realise that your life is going in a different direction."

As if to prove the point, Angus loaded me with new musical responsibilities. There were duets with Seamus, a new round of RAM examinations, new choral pieces to accompany. He thought I would help him, as usual, with the orchestra and choir he was conducting for the Henry Wood Promenade

Concerts. He described new roles for me – assistant concertmaster – that in fairer weather would have made me dizzy with excitement, but it was the wrong moment. I was indignant that Fanny's health was not absorbing all his attention. Cancelling concerts was inconceivable to him, and he insisted that I should be there to help. Any of his pupils would have seized the chance to work with him and paid for their own cabs.

I gave in to adult pressure and went back to teaching with James to the end of term. In July when lessons ceased, Angus was obsessed with his musical calendar. Seamus was ready to graduate, and for part of his performance, my uncle was playing the second piano. Seamus's fingers had no calluses, so they often bled during long practices. I thought he lacked the physical strength needed for virtuoso, but I had been forbidden to comment on any aspect of his femininity. Aunty remonstrated with my uncle: "I don't think that boy will amount to much, either. Surely this year you could cancel your concerts."

His refusal was swift and terse. Yet after two recitals in Brighton, Seamus caught measles and became so ill that he withdrew from all engagements. My uncle decided I would play the Mozart piano duets with him. I argued that I was under-rehearsed, and I wanted to stay home, but the matter was decided by Fanny, who was tired of her father's restless prowling. She told him to buy the expensive tickets for us to hear Elgar's debut as conductor of the London Symphony Orchestra, in exchange for five nights of my help in Brighton.

As soon as I began to work with my uncle in Brighton it was clear that both the orchestra and choir were under-rehearsed, and his work had been slipping for the last six months. The sopranos were a trial. Musicians were missing, along with 20 music stands and some rented brass instruments. Two soloists became combative, shrieking about hair pieces and cloaks. The piano was out of tune. The wrong scores had been sent. The company was in chaos and my notebooks overflowed with instructions, timetables, venues, piano tuners. There were 40 voices to be assigned places, and too many were unable to read their parts without coaching. I listened for the confident voices to lead each section, but most women clung to their friends who were invariably flat. Some contraltos were improvising. Each day I became more irritated with the choir. The singers were more than twice my age, but they were excitable, chattering through every break, interrupting with inane questions and observations. They were amateurs who only sang in the holidays, and they regarded it as their jolliest social outing of the year. The professional soloists were outraged by the amateur's disruptions.

Everything changed when we returned to London. Familiar singers joined us, and most were trained. It rarely took more than an afternoon to resolve problems with broken piano strings and a missing musician. Attendance at our concerts was often poor, but the conviviality of the company made their efforts worthwhile. At the end of an evening, Angus invited the orchestra and singers home for a drink. While I lay awake calculating our indebtedness to piano tuners, Angus was downstairs noisily attending to his sopranos. One night I went out to the landing in annoyance. Aunty was standing further along the hallway with a candle.

"Can't you tell him to send them all home?" I pleaded. "Poor Fanny needs sleep."

"Have some pity, Kate," she replied. "He needs the company. They won't wake Fanny, because she has taken a sleeping draught."

Near dawn there were people downstairs still singing nostalgic fragments. I could imagine the women's fluttering eyelashes and the subtle glares of contempt between rivals. I heard my uncle's voice slurry with alcohol, probably absorbed in trivialities and flattery. I was anxious for the end of the season. It should have been such a triumph for me, working with Angus at this level. I knew some of his boys envied me, but I could not pretend to be satisfied.

On the final night of the promenade there was an atmosphere of confident anticipation among the company. We were performing a much-loved Latin mass, Faure's Requiem, a favourite of my uncle, despite his anti-Catholic theology. The Queen's Hall had a capacity audience, which inspired the performers. I was seated nervously at the piano before the curtain went up, when Angus came up behind me and squeezed my shoulders. I caught my breath, wanting words that would give me courage.

"You are not playing for me as your teacher," he said. "You are performing because you have earned the right."

The audience was captivated, and they seemed to collectively cease breathing, the stillness broken only by the gentle flight of my hands. The unearthly ambience restrained me, and my touch was lighter than it had been for weeks, my emotions caught up only in the music. In my side vision I glanced to the wings. Angus had a triumphant smile of pride and approbation. He had reclaimed ground and erased any memory of the bumbling performances in

Brighton. As the piano faded away, he mounted the podium, his eyes travelling slowly along the ranks of the orchestra, a small smile of reassurance on his lips as he demanded their focus. Then he raised himself to his full height and swept us away with his baton, into a glorious flow of orchestration. It was remarkable. I sensed the exhilaration of the orchestra. The audience responded with razor sharp concentration, eyes fixed and bodies motionless throughout the theatre. When it was over the silence last for three seconds before the explosive applause assured us, we had excelled.

Afterwards, the choir and orchestra began to unwind into a party, loud and spontaneous. I heard corks popping and glasses clinking. I knew we had to leave the building soon, so I waited on a bench in the hallway, unable to face idle chatter. About twenty minutes elapsed before the noise began to subside. There was a queue of cabs outside, and people were hurrying to collect their coats. I went back into the supper room to look for Angus, and caught a glimpse of him from behind, just as his hand slipped into the small of the back of one of the choristers. It was a recalcitrant contralto, so inexperienced that her inclusion had troubled me. She was wearing an insolent sweeping purple gown, a white shawl slipping from her plump shoulders. She took his hand, and he willingly followed her down a darkened staircase.

I returned to the bench, furious. He had abandoned me, and he was ignoring the crisis at home, to pursue a woman without substance. I composed speeches to hold him to account for his negligence. I rehearsed what I would say to Aunty. I ached for home and to know Fanny was just sleeping. It was an interminable wait in the bitter cold. Half an hour went by, and the hallways were empty by the time he reappeared, flustered. The woman had gone. Without explanation he went out and whistled down a lone cab, and I got in, grateful only that we did not need to walk. I sat shivering in my coat as far from Angus as the carriage allowed. When he offered me an overcoat that was covering his knees, I did not move.

"Not speaking to me then, Kate? What have I done?"

"You are totally immoral," I said indignantly.

He was silent for a long time before snapping back impatiently: "Good Lord, Kate. If you want to be ornery and critical, let me say you were a brilliant pianist this season, but nobody's friend. You were bad tempered, arrogant, prickly, rude, irritated, and tonight you could not take five minutes to celebrate with everyone. All night I have been fielding questions about who has offended you. You have offended everyone with your brusque manner. I am offended. You might be competent musically to play at Queen's Hall, but you must grow up and develop some compassion for people. You cannot lead people unless you develop some fellow feelings for them."

I was battered by his words. Usually, only alcohol unleashed his mood, but he had not been drinking. That made it worse, because he was never so transparently condemnatory of anyone.

I retaliated with contempt: "I saw you go down the stairs with one of the singers."

"Oh," he replied with a laugh. "Kate, I am an unmarried man. Don't be my keeper. Don't judge me. I am a grown-up. You can't chastise me. Aunty is right, I've ruined your good nature. I am not going to defend your dreadful manners anymore. If you choose to be a shrew, then you can suffer the consequences. Is there anyone left in the world that you approve of, or even like?"

"The only person I care about in the world today is Fanny," I whispered hoarsely. "I never wanted to leave her for these concerts. I did not want to stay out celebrating while Fanny is at home dying."

He was startled. He shuddered. Ten minutes passed before he spoke again.

"God love you Kate," he said, his voice breaking. "God love you. Your heart is in the right place. I heard you play magnificently tonight. If only you had heard the consolation of Faure."

Consolation? There was no escaping my fear. The dense fog swirled around the cab until we could see nothing except the feint glow of streetlights. The cab swished slowly along the damp road, and beyond my window London was still, the world vanishing from sight. Angus did not contradict my assessment that Fanny was dying. There was no elation in the music, no jubilation in going home to the gracious place Miss Po had invented for us. I no longer felt significant in sharing a cab home with the professor. I had no joy in what we had achieved. It was an elusive fantasy. Fanny was mortally ill, and even Angus, for all his relentless optimism, would no longer deny it.

7

The Bogey Man Cometh

Fanny died two weeks later. The end came so swiftly that I thought there had been no warning. Autumn had blustered in. There were no children in James's school because the change of season had brought chills. Unexpectedly, Fanny wanted to get out of bed and go to school. For a moment she seemed strong and determined. She walked easily to Parmiter, holding Aunty's arm. As soon as she sat at her desk, her legs were heavy and her breathing a trial. Aunty decided to stay until Fanny was breathing steadily. James was in a mellow mood, and he was glad to have Aunty's company, chatting with her for almost another hour before she went home.

When Fanny developed a headache, I presumed it was just the seasonal sickness and the overheated room. I was busy, so I hardly registered the progression of her complaints, from blurred to double vision, a churning stomach, nausea, a dry mouth, and her heart fluttering away, fast and loud. Then she started labouring for air. James opened the door, and a cool breeze swept through. Fanny dropped her head onto her arms, and I thought she was snoring, until James scuttled across the room, alarmed, and said: "Those breathing sounds are worrying me." We stood silently together, listening. After each tortured breath there was a long pause. We held our own breath.

"Go and fetch Gus," James said, his voice rasping. "Run, please. Run, Kate."

Angus carried her home, but the crisis seemed to pass. By teatime Fanny was laying limply in her father's lap, her eyes swollen, a cold flannel across her forehead, the curtains drawn against the light, waiting for Dr Broadhurst. Aunty had drawn up a Chippendale chair and she was reading in a barely audible tone. At the top of the stairs, I announce my arrival when I tossed my brown leather briefcase so it landed with a good thump on the landing. Fanny opened one eye and wiggled three fingers weakly in greeting. That gesture made it seem such an ordinary afternoon. Angus lowered her into her bed, kissed her forehead, and tucked the quilt around her shoulders. I wanted them to go away so I could climb in bed with Fanny and talk nonsense to make the day go away. Outside the room, Jess dozed against the landing rail. Pearl came into the bedroom and climbed into Aunty's lap, pushed a shrivelled thumb into her mouth, and fell asleep instantly to the drone of words.

"Don't come into my bed," Fanny said, guessing my intent. "My body hurts too much to be touched." The general somnolence of the room irritated me. I went downstairs to make toast. I still had tea in my Toby jug when Angus came loping in.

"Can I drain your teacup?" he asked.

"I'll make you a fresh one," I offered.

"Just a mouthful is all I want," he said, swilling down my lukewarm dregs. "Do you want to come for a walk?"

"No, I want to sit with Fanny. She didn't want me."

"She sent me out, too. Aunty is with her."

I had a surge of energy that needed to be expended and an aching desire to run.

"I'll get my coat," I said.

We covered a couple of miles without words, until the sky darkened, and the night crept over us so quickly that I felt an ominous wave of anxiety. I wanted to turn towards home, but Angus wanted to buy a bottle of malt whisky from the *White Hart*, because James was coming over. We walked through a flurry of unseasonal snow near Clapton Pond where a small crowd was gathering for an event. We could hear the bell pads of some Morris Men, tinkling as they waited under a gas light. A piper was playing, chestnuts were roasting, and vendors were setting up their stoves and stalls. My uncle slowed his pace, curious and willing to linger. Oil lamps were glowing over the stalls. We stood against the fence, absorbed by the dissonance of the night. Angus rested his arm around my shoulder, but it was no great weight any longer. I was mildly surprised to check my height against his, not certain whether he was shrinking, or I really had grown to such a great height.

"Aren't you in a hurry to go home?" I asked. He did not answer. When I looked directly into the web of fine crinkles around his eyes, I realised something was amusing him.

"Fanny," he said softly.

I nodded, knowing Fanny was on our minds, even we were too afraid to speak her name.

"I am surprised I can laugh when she is so poorly," he said.

"You're laughing about Fanny?" I asked. "Are you going to tell me what was so funny?"

"Oh yes," he said. "She made me laugh about you."

We had not had an uncomplicated conversation in weeks. All the lines of his face were arced in secret amusement. He was speaking in his teasing voice, which I had almost forgotten. I tugged at his arm to demand more information.

"Fanny told me you paid those barrow boys. Those rogues who said they burned down the church," he said. "Ten shillings stolen from my money jar."

I felt the telltale colour rising on my cheeks, but his amusement increased until he was laughing out loud: "Aye, Katy Elliot. I found that hard to believe, but clearly it is true. What a blush you have! Thank God you are blushing. You robbed me of ten shillings."

"Why are you laughing? You didn't tell the truth about that fire, either," I said. "The police came. You and the others were locked up in prison for a couple of weeks. They obviously did not believe a German combustion stove set fire to the rector's house."

My uncle hesitated. He patted his own warm cheeks and laughed out loud again, "We red-heads give ourselves away," he said. I watched his awkward evasion until he relented and added cautiously: "It was a suffragette thing. The fire alerted the police to Dr Stowe being in that house with a few others."

"I never did believe those boys caused the fire," I said defensively. "Fanny wanted to believe them."

He shrugged. "I think she still believes it. I should not be amused, because she was very earnest, worrying that it might be the unforgiveable sin, burning down a church," he said. He inspected his shoes and the back of one hand, and then turned to me with a tight smile: "You are a loyal friend to Fanny. I appreciate that so much, in all our difficulties, you have been unwavering in your loyalty to Fanny. You can take ten shillings off me any time you like."

I hooked my arm through his, because it still gave me a sense of safety and peace. I no longer imagined he could protect us against the impending catastrophe.

"I really want to go home and sit with Fanny, now. She needs me to read to her to keep the bogey man away."

He nodded solemnly: "The bogey man cometh, Kate. I am not sure we can chase him away for much longer."

Twenty minutes later we returned to the stillness of a cold house. The moment we entered the atrium,

I sensed an absence. Mrs Lloyd caught sight of us coming in. She turned, and I glimpsed her scurrying back to the dining room, her hair undone and her eyes red. I had seen that sight before, when I was ten years old, watching in horror as Dotty's tears flowed, her hair escaping from her cap in ripples of protest. My uncle latched the door, alert to the strange ambience, and we stood expectantly, listening. There was a rumble of low voices in the dining room. The door clicked open. Dr Broadhurst appeared first, ashen and grim, followed in agonised slow motion by James and Aunty, their faces etched with pain, their eyes screaming something that my uncle instantly understood. I knew it, too, but my mind rebelled against its own intuition.

"She has gone. There was nothing more I could do. Her poor heart just faded away, my dear man," the doctor said softly. "I am so profoundly sorry."

The whisky bottle slipped from my uncle's hand and shattered on the flagstones at our feet. His knees buckled, but the doctor caught his elbow and kept him upright. My uncle's gracious manners did not desert him.

"Thank you," he said, clasping Dr Broadhurst's limp hand. "I know you did everything you could."

Then he pushed past the doctor and ran up the stairs two at a time. Someone was holding my arm, so I could not follow. I heard an animal cry coming from the room I had once shared with Fanny. We stood in a little wordless circle. Aunty was staring down at the puddle of broken glass as the warm aroma of the whisky rose around us. Mrs Lloyd was back with a broom, equally baffled by the broken glass. Everyone seemed confused and the doctor looked at me helplessly. Another dreadful howl echoed into the void, and before I could decide whether it was man or beast, I saw five fat ginger cats coming down the stairs slowly, in a single line, yowling their distress. It was James's clawed hand that was attached to my arm, and I pulled away slowly, until the claw slid down to my wrist. I tried to shake him off, but his grip was strong.

"Kate," he said. "Stay here."

"Why are you holding me? Let me go," I said.

"Fanny has just died," James said, his hoarse voice slamming against the silence.

"Yes, I realise that," I said coldly. "Now let go of my arm so that I can go and see her."

"It's not your place to go up there," he said.

"It's not your place to stop me," I shouted.

Aunty's wide worn hands settled on James's shoulder, and we both looked at her in alarm, like children caught wrestling.

"Kate, I am going to need you to help me up the stairs. We will go and see Fanny together. But let's just give Angus a few moments by himself."

Her voice was too reasonable to be contradicted.

Fanny was buried on Thursday. The house was subdued. The piano was silent. Pearl retrieved the cats one at a time and moved them to the nursery. Jess was untouched by the absence of her twin. When I said that I would go to Abney Park for the committal, there was no opposition. Aunty said she would come too. No women in her family had ever been to the graveside. We both thought the funeral was a barren ritual. Mr Robart intoned God words that were like autumn leaves, crackling, disintegrating, scattering. The bright spring days when Fanny danced down the lane, were over. Fanny would not have enjoyed this ceremony, but thankfully, we had never talked about it. The death bed scene she had planned, and craved, had been a travelling circus that lasted weeks. So many people called on her during the long faltering of her heart, and I was glad she had enjoyed holding court.

The old Clarence from my grandfather's garage was put into service under the control of a uniformed chauffeur. Marriot did not attend. Aunty and James watched the burial while sitting in the elegant carriage, which had been buffed to a shine for the occasion. Marriot had supplied two well matched horses that were plumed in black dyed ostrich feathers from the last century. I recalled that feathers, despised by suffragettes, were once worth a pound apiece. Four men unknown to me lowered the small coffin into the heaving mud, and took a few shillings each from Nort, who had taken charge of this aspect of the ceremony. When the group was ready to disperse, my legs were weak. Mr Robart pressed me to get into the carriage with Aunty, his hand intruding upon my back. I pulled away from him repeatedly. I resented all these old people who were alive when Fanny was dead. Aunty called out: "Please leave her, thank you Reverend Robart. She is in familiar territory. Kate will find her own way home when she is ready."

I was appalled to see Fanny's ghastly resting place. I was standing motionless, overcome by the reality of death, when a muted sound made me glance up to see Angus, shaking off Mr Robart's trespassing hands. The priest went back to the carriage on the gravel road, his head down, his cassock sweeping the earth. The carriage wheels crunched away through the iron gates. Angus returned to the graveside and closed his eyes. He placed his Homburg firmly on his head and then he held out his hands, his palms up, in a gesture of supplication I had never witnessed before. An unrestrained note of grief suddenly came out of his chest, but it was instantly transformed into a pure note that found its melody. He was singing. It echoed through the tombstones. I saw artisans halt in the distance, look back from some headstones they were erecting, and listen intently. He captured the sound into a melodic descent that I recognised. He unleashed his voice, its resonance full of the East and the synagogue. He was singing Hebrew words that were vaguely familiar to me. Then he sang the English words of Job 19, which I had heard so often in Handel's oratorio. The strength of his voice in that open space was hypnotic. I could not recall him ever singing in full voice like this. He was the one who released the voices of others. Then he began again in Hebrew, perhaps the twenty-second psalm. Finally, he rejoined our dissenter ancestors and lapsed into a metrical chant that went on for several minutes before he was finally silent. This was coming from the depths of his unorthodox beliefs. This was passion and not performance. His voice was equal to the outrage Abney Park represented for me. This was Fanny's moment, the sound of her father's voice loaded with the fury and faith that had been missing from the funeral service. He sang for Fanny alone. I stood watching in wonder because he seemed to derive an inscrutable power from his vacillating god. The atmosphere of the dark cemetery changed with his songs. I felt a rush of joy for the life we had lived together, we sisters, even if it was over. I felt thankful for Fanny's brief life. Her tired heart no longer struggled to live. She did not have to make sense of the griefs of life. She did not have to spend forty years building something beautiful, filling it with people to love, to have it shattered by arbitrary fate, to be alone again. My fear of futility gave way, for a moment, to peace.

The workers had sensed it was a sacred song, and they removed their caps, and stood, heads bowed, their shovels at rest. When Angus finished singing, the shovels started up again, scraping harshly against stones, breaking sod in the distance. Angus turned to leave, and he was surprised to find me still there.

"Ahh, aha, Kate. You waited for me. Thankyou."

"Why did you do that?" I asked, genuinely interested in what I had observed. "Sing? Here."

He looked at the gathering clouds and smiled into the distance: "Fanny died with so much of her music inside of her. I will make music for her for the rest of my life," he said.

We walked without a word. It was a strange, unsettled afternoon. There had been a brief shower, and the damp roads were quiet, except for the occasional swish of a bicycle. A storm rumbled in the distance, and the rustling of the trees brought silence to the birds. Far away a dog was barking spasmodic warnings at the blackened sky. Normally we would dash if rain threatened, but today it was a long slow walk. Nort was following fifty yards behind, his hat still in his hand. As we turned into Morning Lane, I wondered why there was a line of motors at the kerb near our house. On the opposite side of the road there were carriages. I sighed, wearied to realise I had seen these motors and carriages before. All the relations I had not seen since my parents' deaths, had come to mourn a girl they never knew.

8
Farewell Morning Lane

Without Fanny, the house was just a chasm. Her eighth and final tapestry for the dining room chairs was still in its frame. Aunty said she needed courage to complete it. I needed courage to go through with my plan to leave Morning Lane. I went up to the bedroom I had shared with Fanny, to pack my clothes, and Agnes willingly carried my boxes to the atrium. The cats returned cautiously to inspect Fanny's bed. It was stripped to the wire. Just as the cats began to curl together on a pile of Fanny's abandoned nightdresses on the floor, Pearl marched in, pink with annoyance, followed by Aunty, who was curious about my activities.

"Fanny told the cats they would belong to me when she went," Pearl announced. "But I don't think they understand."

"Let's take all the cats out of here again and shut this door," I said.

"Are you packing up Fanny's things," Aunty asked, puzzled at my haste. "I saw some luggage downstairs."

"Those are mine," I said. "I'm moving to my grandfather's."

A flash of anger crossed her craggy face. She suppressed her retort and stamped off to her own room. I was glad that she had chosen to ignore me for a little while. I was not ready to explain that I felt redundant. Morning Lane no longer felt like home. My decision had been developing for months. It had only taken a week after Fanny's death for me to resolve it was time to leave. My grandfather was not surprised when I asked if I could move into his house. He cautiously offered to let me have two rooms, a carriage and driver, and a maid. I was stunned at his estimation of my needs. He cast me as a Victorian lady, rather than a child who had happily occupied half of a mouldy little room.

"My sister will give me the rounds of the kitchen for this," he lamented. "But you have lost your closest companion. You need a change of landscape."

When Aunty thought she was ready for a discussion, she called me down to the breakfast room for tea. She waited quietly until I had finished practising a piece, and I went and sat with her, where a teacup had been set for me, empty, yet full of meaning. Aunty's eyelids batted at a great pace as she struggled with her anxiety. I was sorry to be a disappointment to her because she had proven a good ally.

"You don't know Marriot," she said firmly. "He likes to be alone. He will make you lonely."

"I enjoy his company," I said. "He knows I'm not going to teach for James anymore."

"But James does not know that," she protested.

We stared at our teacups wordlessly, embattled but unarmed. After a few minutes Aunty added: "James's health is deteriorating. The school can't go on for much longer."

"I can't go on. I am worn out," I said.

"We all are. Grief makes us all very tired. What about your piano pupils?" she countered.

"I have lost interest in the piano. I want to get away from it."

"Can you imagine what that will do to Angus?" she said angrily. "After all Angus has done for you, and all the hopes he has for you. He loves you like a daughter. You will break his heart. He has just lost Fanny. And now you are going."

Pearl had been sitting quietly in the corner with her dolls when she heard the portent of our conversation. "You can't go Kate," she shouted in protest. "I won't have any sisters left. I am telling papa. He will stop you." Pearl leapt up and screamed as she ran through the house, "Papa papa Kaaateeee is going, too. Tell her she can't go. What about me? Why are they leaving me? Who is going to look after me? Papa. Papa."

Aunty went after her. I filled my teacup, thankful to be alone with my thoughts. Minutes later my uncle bellowed my name several times, volume increasing steadily. I went to the studio door, steeling myself to hold my course. He was at the piano, cleaning between the keys with a small brush, and he did not look up.

"What is going on, Katy Elliot?" he asked. "There is pandemonium out there with wailing women. Why is everyone shouting? I thought you were just going for tea with Marriot. Pearl says you are leaving us. What am I missing? Have I done something wrong again?"

"You let James treated us very badly."

"He is a good teacher. Just a bit strict."

"He killed Fanny."

Angus rose abruptly, the crevices of his face deep and dark with rage. For an instant I thought he would slap me. Instead, as his eyes met mine, his fury swiftly retreated to the limits of his Christian principles. He was a fearful sight when his temper was provoked, but he did not intimidate me. I knew my fears belonged in Parmiter, and not in this house. Angus was able to overwhelm his temper, bite down on his words. I wondered if the unreliable aspects of Angus in the last few months, were anguish and grief. I wondered if my own volatility came from the same source.

"Fanny's health problems began long before James came," he assured me. "She was attacked by her own heart. He did nothing worse than be her friend. He sat with her to her last breath."

I gasped out loud: "Was he actually with Fanny when she died."

"He was."

"I should have been here."

"It was not my plan, Kate. But I am glad you were not here."

I wanted to ask why, but bouts of panic had been plaguing me, so that I could not speak. It was too painful to hear that James was with Fanny when she died. I felt envy, anger, betrayal, exclusion, and I could not ask Fanny to explain why she had allowed it. If James wanted to hurt me, he had succeeded again. If Angus had wanted to lacerate my heart, he had the weapon. Here was Angus defending James again. There was no guile in his words, but every time he had compassion for James, I felt torn down. My emotions were rioting. I was glad I was leaving. I was glad this would hurt him. When my breath returned, I retaliated with resentment: "You promised to protect me from Aunty," I said fiercely.

"Did I?" he asked. "Why would you need protecting from poor old Aunty?"

"She cooked up this school with James and you just let her. We had an agreement that you would develop my musical education, and I would not have to go to grammar school. This was worse. You did not control her at all."

Aunty appeared at the doorway, probably at the sound of her own name.

"Well, I am controlling you," he said, mostly for Aunty's benefit. "This is your home, and you are my daughter, and you are not going anywhere."

"But I am not your daughter."

"I am not talking about biology. You know I have done my best to be a good father to you," he said. "Out of respect for your elders you should ask my permission before you make plans to run off someplace".

"You have never expected me to ask permission for anything."

"How right you are," Aunty said.

We both turned to glare at Aunty, alarmed by her imposing, uninvited presence. Her shoulders went back defensively: "This is upon your own head, Angus. This is what you get for being so indulgent, letting Kate get on the tram and go into the West End on the cross-bar of a bicycle at night."

He snapped at her sharply: "My bicycle. My bicycle. I told you she only ever went on my bicycle, not the boys." And with that he jumped up and slammed the door in her face. I guessed they had been rowing privately. The fury he restrained for my sake had been expended on her. I had unleashed a storm. I needed him to return to his good disposition again. It was his reliable nature that allowed me to speak my mind. There was so much I wanted to say and needed to know. I watched the landscape of his face moving in concert with his emotions. His high colour was like a fading sunset, and his eyes finally came back to me.

"Katy," he said. "This is about Fanny. If I could have done anything to change the course of her life, don't you think I would have done so?"

I was instantly in tears, embarrassed by my emotions: "No, it's not," I insisted. "It's James and that school."

"It is the loss of Fanny for all of us. Nothing else," he said. "We are all at sixes and sevens. It will take us months to find our way again."

"No," I said. But it was a useless gasp of protest because I was crying too much.

"You cannot know how sorry I am that you have suffered this terrible loss. You two girls were inseparable. But please, I am asking you to not add to our grief. Leaving this house is no answer. Pearl is asleep with exhaustion from crying for fear you are going. She needs you. I need you."

"Pearl will be fine. She thinks my going is the same as Fanny's going. She just needs to understand I will be staying in another house," I said.

"I told her that Fanny was staying in a mansion in the sky," he said guiltily.

I groaned: "How could you say that. No wonder Pearl is confused. You hardly go to church anymore."

"But I do believe Fanny is in heaven, where God is. The Lord doesn't live in churches."

"He doesn't live in the picture rails, either," I said.

He puzzled for a moment, then spluttered into laughter. It broke the tension.

"Kate, let's forget our quarrels and try to get back to normal. I've already talked to Miss Po about building a second studio for you and your pupils."

"No. Don't make any more plans for my life, please. I am too young to have my whole life mapped out for me. I don't want to be playing any more God music. God never helped us. I was out chaperoning an aging lothario and suffering trial by sopranos all summer when I wanted to be here with Fanny. She wanted me here with her."

He was weeping shamelessly when he whispered: "Fanny did not want you to see her suffer. If we were in that room, she felt she could not leave her mortal body to go to God."

That was the slap. I moved to the piano stool where he could not see my tears. In an instant my fingers released my taut emotions and flew across the keys, shaping sounds like a river dispersing gently, falling away to a trickle. I found a new rush of chords that sustained a river until it gathered strength, then crashed down through the lashers.

"Kate," Angus said. "I wish you would give me some more time to bring your musicianship into full bloom. You owe me that."

"I owe you? Haven't I done enough work for you in this house?"

The moment I spoke, I regretted my words. It was an echo of my father's voice raging at Parmiter, his bitter resentment of an unspecified debt to Marriot, constantly repaid in compliance and respect. Angus said: "Don't misunderstand me. I am only asking you for more time. We have lost the last year, and truth be told, yes, I lost time to James's project. I meant that we need to make up lost time. I only want what I thought you wanted for yourself. Excellence."

I felt my defences crumbling. "I am not ungrateful for all you have done," I said.

"I don't want gratitude. I have been trying to repay gratitude of my own. You know my parents died destitute," he said. "Aunty and Marriot gave me and your father an education that was unimaginable to the Elliots in their little fishing village of Gamrie, in Scotland. Education is the most important armament in life. Nothing you learn is ever wasted, not even sacred music. I was grateful to pass that on to you."

I knew gratitude was the deep well that motivated my uncle's generosity. My father's experience of charity, although identical, had led to misery. This insight did not help me understand myself in the turmoil of the moment. I needed to leave, and I had no words to justify myself.

"I cannot stay here," I said, my voice barely audible. "Not without Fanny."

Angus scanned the picture rail and looked out longingly at the dismal day, then he looked at me intently, as though God had just supplied his script.

"Of course," he sighed. "If this is what you need to do, go with my blessing. This will always be your home, and you will always be a child of mine. You will do your grandfather good. He's too much alone."

He was at peace, and I envied him for it. Smiling, he pointed towards his teaching violin: "I want you to take the Gagliano with you. You won't have a piano. I don't care if you play Elgar. But please, you need to play something, just for your own sake."

"I can't take that violin. You love that instrument."

"I intended to give it to you if you became my concertmaster," he said, still smiling. "That was my plan for next year when you turn eighteen. I repent of planning your life."

"Don't make me feel guilty, please."

"The Gagliano is yours. Enjoy it," he said. "It's the gift of an aging lothario to a girl who has been my inspiration to persevere in teaching these last few years."

He packed the Gagliano into its leather case, and he pushed it against me hard until I grudgingly took hold of it.

"Oh, oh, and take this..." he said, laughing out loud.

There was a thick envelope under his music folio. It was handmade paper, stained in blotches of bright colours that bled into clots of crude fibrous swirls - something made by Pearl in the nursery. My name was stitched in a patch of perfect petit point - entwined hearts – attached to the envelope. Fanny's work. The envelope was heavy with sovereigns. I unfolded a letter in Fanny's hand, which said: *Birthday money to buy Katy a red coat.*

"Fanny took that money off James, playing cards," Angus said. "She found her own way to make him pay for all those detentions. You should buy your own coat and wear it while it's still chilly, rather than wait for your birthday."

He laughed, kissed me and said in his deepest brogue, "Will y' nay come back again? Aye, surely, thou wilt return."

A song or a poem? I would not ask.

"Oh Lord," he said to the picture rail, "I must make peace with my aunt. That will take three cups of tea."

9
The Red Coat

I bought the red coat at Harrods. The coat was the most insolent red in London. I was wearing it when I ran into the family in Oxford Street, on their way home from a Saturday matinee. Angus was so impressed that he gave me two pounds to buy a matching bonnet. Even Aunty admired my coat, but she leaned in to whisper that she imagined Marriot was not proving to be colourful company. He was not, but I would not give Aunty any satisfaction by concurring.

Months later, I wore my red coat and bonnet to Abney Park to see Fanny's headstone set. Fanny's grave was parallel to the unknown child, Florence Maud Elliot, and the headstones were identical in design. It was not a coincidence. Angus had been very insistent when he invited me to the stone setting. I was determined to make no comment, ask no questions, but as we were leaving, Angus came and tentatively reached for my hand.

"It was right that these two girls should lay together," he said.

"Are you about to tell me why that is the case?" I asked, smiling.

"A long time ago you were very curious about this unknown child. Do you recall?"

"Oh yes, I certainly do," I said.

"It was genuinely a mystery to me. Some of my aunts said that Marriot put the headstone up. I could not make any sense of it."

"Do you know now?" I asked.

"Yes. Marriot admitted he had the headstone erected here for Florence Maud," he said. "Has anyone told you about this?"

"My grandfather has not mentioned it to me."

"His mind is foggy," he said.

"But why did he do it?" I asked.

"Ah, yes. Surely you do not want the full story?" he teased.

I punched his arm, laughing, startled to find myself coltish at Fanny's graveside.

"Someone sent Marriot a letter saying there was a child buried in an unmarked grave in the family plot," he said, regaining his solemnity. "The cemetery records proved the child's name and gravesite. The letter named me as her father. I realised, from the date, that she may indeed have been mine. Before I was married, I was put out of the church for immorality."

I nodded. "Fanny told me you had a girlfriend in Scotland," I said.

"This child was born after my liaison in Scotland," he said. "I knew nothing about her on the day we first stood here and saw the headstone. I certainly did not bury the child here. I can't even tell what happened to her, because the mother clearly wanted to keep her secret. I hope you believe me, Kate."

"Of course, I believe you Uncle Gus," I said, disturbed by his need for my approval. "Did you think I would despise you for things that happened so long ago?"

"I wondered. You made such an awful accusation about my morality before you left Morning Lane. It was true. It has plagued me. This affair had just come back to haunt me, and I realised I was still the same immoral man. That is what you saw and despised. I should not have driven you out of my house with my double standards. I thought I was a better man."

"That was not why I left," I said firmly. "I could not be in that house without Fanny."

"You had the right to say those things," he said.

"There are things I said that I regret."

"There are things I have done that I regret," he said.

Nothing more needed to be said to repair our walls. We were both suffering guilt and regret. I realised the truth of Aunty's frequent, grim pronouncements: the passionate overflow of my creativity was as troublesome to me as everything I observed so critically in Angus. I understood his loneliness, now. I understood how the exhilaration of making music met so many needs. I had already fallen into the deep gulf of reality where the music ceased.

"I only wish Fanny knew about this," I sighed, pointing to the twin graves. "She desperately wanted to know who Florence Maud was."

"She knew," he said happily. "I told her not long before she died. She had guessed some of it. I intended to tell you, but she had other plans. So, she managed to keep the secret?"

"She did," I said, surprised.

"It was her idea to have these matching headstones."

I kissed him. "You are a good father," I said. "I am so glad Fanny heard the end of the story. I am so glad you told her. I know how hard it is for you when we want to go poking into the past."

"I had enough strife from the gossiping old aunts," he said.

"I wonder if we will ever find out why they imagine – well, you know what they imagine."

"The red hair," he laughed. "And you growing to six feet tall. Aunts and gossip!"

I walked regretfully to my grandfather's Brougham, where the chauffeur was smoking a pipe as he waited. I jiggled home to the house where I lived, but I did not belong. All my emotions churned together, happy and sad, but no longer obsessed with secrets and lies. When truth finally emerged it seemed obvious, and yet facile, because the absence of truth had already created a whirlwind of lies. The value of transparency popped into my mind as the carriage drove into the courtyard at Hampstead, and I decided this would be the first of my life's principles.

My grandfather came out, delighted to see I had been at the stone setting in such a bright costume. He hated the drab colours of mourning and all its rituals. When I said I had few opportunities to wear my coat and bonnet, he offered to discuss with Miss Po how we might rectify that. I hoped he would not. Although I was missing concerts and theatre, I felt slightly concerned that Miss Po would have an opportunity to observe that the serviceable houndstooth coat had been abandoned in a cupboard at Morning Lane.

I wandered aimlessly at my grandfather's house. I missed the Guild Hall, my uncle's boys, even the Saturday walks in London that had punctuated our life at Morning Lane. It would have been too audacious to ask either of my uncles to pay conservatorium fees, after the choices I had made to abandon them. When I walked on the heath with the Gagliano I tried to appear purposeful. My grandfather's driver followed at a distance, my perpetual chaperone. When I played the beautiful violin, I stood beside the pond, allowing my mood to guide the bow. Usually, I only played for half an hour before I gave in to self-pity and cried. My grandfather's few comments at dinner made it obvious that he saw my sorry state, and he thought I needed to do something useful with my life.

I yearned to see Jess and Pearl, but I was determined to not go back to Morning Lane and face my failed ambitions and tempestuous bad choices. I was also avoiding the reproach of Aunty and her factotums. Her contempt for my decision to move out had not abated. I suspected she only wrote to me regularly to remind me that I had thumbed my nose at the entire family, including Poor Jimmy. I could barely admit to myself that I craved the intellectual challenges that James had set for me. My grandfather's library of great books was useless to me without guidance. Yet if I ever thought about James, I stirred up my rage. I still thought that he had toadied his way into Aunty's concerns and stolen Fanny's affections. I was repulsed by the memory of him.

I considered putting my name down to attend a high school to complete matriculation, perhaps aiming towards a women's college at Oxford. I knew that would redeem me in Aunty's estimation. Yet I had no energy for it. My strength was being spent on regrets. All the unshed tears of childhood, finally liberated, poured out at the wrong moments. I hated my perpetually red-eyed sour mood, but I could not make it lift. Colden Bridge haunted my dreams, filled me with dread and panic, leapt into my waking moments and led me to consider what my life might have been like, if only my mother, father and brother, had lived. The family I lost became a fantasy indulged for long hours, between weeping and worrying and being half asleep with sorrow. Each day I became more bitter. I had not only lost Fanny, but I had also lost my substitute family. I had walked away from them. I had abandoned the best aspects of the life I had created at Morning Lane out of revenge or spite. I had not suffered this depth of sorrow when I was younger, but now my grief was a pile of muddled sheet music, and nothing made sense. My fury was directed at God, and then, at Angus, as the person nearest to God that I knew. I felt Fanny had fallen into the deceptions of his religion, and she had relinquished her life too easily. Yet even that was not true. I tossed all night long and then slept until noon.

My grandfather was awkward with me. His fractured memories spoiled conversation. He retold his stories of people and places I did not know. He offered snippets of information about the problems of strangers, mostly his poor tenants. He pontificated on the sloth of the poor. He regarded me as his guest, and he seemed bewildered by my continuing presence. He frequently mentioned how much I was missed at Morning Lane, offering me his regular letters from Aunty that varied little from the ones she sent me. As soon as he felt he had completed the obligatory daily information exchange, he dashed off to his club or the

Holborn office, to avoid me until supper. His insights into my state of mind were surprisingly astute. Yet he suffered the same confusion that I saw in Dotty at the end of her life. Moments of clarity were interrupted by unrelated thoughts. His most eloquent statements were eclipsed suddenly by vanishing words.

"I know about grief," he said reassuringly. "Old people do not recover. Young people have more bounce-back. Although they're mostly dead now, my children."

Two years earlier he had mapped generations of the family for me. Now he could not recall his sisters' names. I had become an unsatisfactory reminder of his lost children, and he often forgot how I fit into his family. I was like a ghost of his lost daughters.

"Goodness me, it's you, young Kate. I thought that was one of my wives coming down the stairs," he said. "Or daughters. Or one of my lost boys. Without sons to take my name forward, I have no legacy, you know."

"You have James?" I replied.

He shrugged. "Poor lad. You don't get along with him, am I right?"

"You're right," I agreed.

"Difficult boy. Too close to his mother. Never got over losing her. He did not like bouncing around in this big empty house with me. He was never here, always with Maudie, once his mother went."

We had the same ghosts inhabiting our minds. His memory reached back decades before I was born, to the lives my parents had known as children, so they were unrecognisable to me. The dead of my generation were elusive to him.

One evening Marriot came home glowing pink with enthusiasm, waving tickets.

"I have been thinking about you, young Kate, with that red coat and bonnet that needs more excitement than this house can offer. I do not know how you abide the company of an old man and this empty house."

"Concert tickets?" I asked.

"Boat tickets for New York," he said, delighted with his surprise.

"New York?" I repeated the words in wonder, several times.

"Lexington Avenue, Manhattan, to be precise. Very fine apartment," he said.

"Manhattan," I said.

"Do you recall your Aunt Florence?" he asked.

"Of course, I do," I said.

"She has been abandoned by her travelling companion somewhere in Greece. Or was it Egypt?

Anyway, she needs someone to travel home with her. To New York. That's where she lives. I bought her a fine apartment there."

The romance of travelling with my lovely aunt was beyond anything I could envision. A primitive excitement awakened in me. It was a revolutionary solution to my lethargy. Florence leapt into my memory, animated and young, arms locked with my mother, whispering. Then, I remembered that Florence was James's sister. Had they corresponded? What did she know about my recalcitrance in James's school, the conflict and accusations? I comforted myself with the knowledge that James's letters were illegible.

In the long silent pause of my reflection, my grandfather's face had fallen into furrows of disappointed. He mistook my hesitation for refusal.

"Are you afraid of taking a boat?" he asked, concerned.

"No," I said.

"Afraid of travelling?"

"No."

"Perhaps you do not want to leave London and your sisters?"

"No. I don't mind going away."

"You could stay for a whole year in America if you liked. We can find an aunt to chaperone you home again," he suggested hopefully. "The aunts are always travelling."

"Yes," I said firmly. "A year would be excellent. Wonderful."

He glowed when he realised I was agreeing. I knew it was precisely the kind of escape I needed, far away. It answered my aching hiatus. I needed a whole ocean between me and my sorrows. I wanted a new place that would give me anecdotes and status and some whiff of maturity, for when I did, inevitably, return to Morning Lane.

"So, you are saying yes?" he asked.

"Yes, oh yes please. But I need to consult Uncle Gus about this," I said. "I know he's not my guardian, but he has been like a father to me. He wants me to ask his permission when I make decisions."

"Of course, he does. He is a good father. I give him credit for that. But I talked to Gus before I got the tickets. I've even asked Caledonia, as she always has her piece to say, too. They completely agree. You will find you cannot run away from your sorrows, but a big break can give you a new perspective."

"They agreed?" I asked.

"They thought it was a capital idea."

"I am very grateful," I said.

"Please, use my telephone to speak to Gus, to put your mind at rest."

I put my arms around his neck to kiss his cheek, and he beamed.

"Philomena Oroton can sort out clothes and baggage for you. Is there anything I can do for you? Anything you need to know?"

The housekeeper had brought in tea.

"There is something I wanted to ask you," I said, now that I had his full attention.

"Ask away," he said.

"I did wonder if you could tell me about the headstone at Abney Park. You know, the one for Florence Maud Elliot," I said cautiously.

"Who?"

"She's an Elliot baby," I prompted.

He looked puzzled. "I was going to tell you all about New York," he said. "What is this about?"

"I wondered if that baby had something to do with the confusion about me," I said. "Your sisters were confused."

He dipped his ginger biscuits into his tea thoughtfully, and then his face opened up with understanding: "Oh, that. Yes, well I wanted to stop the chatter among my sisters, once and for all. After

Angus took that new girl in, Pearl, my sisters were hammering away at me day and night to know who she was."

"Pearl? She's the Nort's granddaughter."

He said no more for a few minutes, busying himself with hot water and looking irritated as his hand stroked the China cup, testing its temperature.

"But who is her father?" he asked, annoyed.

It had not occurred to me that Pearl's presence in Morning Lane had set off the aunts' perennial chatter about Angus's wandering eyes. It assuaged my own indignation to realise that Pearl, an innocent orphan, was being subjected to the same cruel speculations that had wounded me. Pearl was not a mystery, any more than I was.

"I was asking about the child buried at Abney Park," I reminded him. "Florence Maud Elliot."

"Your father's child."

"No, not my father," I said.

His eyes knotted in confusion: "I mean, Angus's child."

"Yes, she is his child," I agreed.

"I don't know why my sisters were so confused. I agreed with Gus when he wanted the girls buried together in the family plot. I was very happy when they looked like a pair of bookends. Very nice stonework."

The words stung, but the triumph of despatching me to New York had exhausted his sensitivities. He descended into a kedgeree of irrelevant words. He had the disease of the aged, and it was now too difficult to extract complex facts from his memory. I reminded myself that I needed to ask Aunty and Angus a lot of questions before they suffered this affliction.

The housekeeper caught my eye as she came into the room, slowly nodding her head in an encouraging way. When she put down the hot water to top up the tea, she tapped her temple with her forefinger, looking down sadly at Marriot. My grandfather was lost in his tea ritual, hiding in the comfort of confusion. He topped his cup with cold milk and threw a damp half-eaten biscuit back on the plate to signal his annoyance.

"I need hot water," he told the housekeeper. "Bring me hot water."

10
New York

The arrival of Florence caused my grandfather both elation and agitation. She had no affection for her father. Every conversation was twisted with barbed reminders of historical offences. Her hostility towards my grandfather filled me with guilty memories of my last angry days at Morning Lane. Her resentment was so ugly that I decided to go to Morning Lane and make peace with Aunty. It was not necessary. She was so excited by my opportunity to travel that she gave me twenty pounds she had been keeping in a Chinese vase. Then she turned over her mattress to find another paper bag stuffed full of sovereigns, which she gave to me without counting it. She said she would instruct the bank to send me a few pounds each month. Although I felt inexplicably rich, Florence was scathing about the pocket money I had been given: "Tight wads we call them. Did you get anything out of James? Make sure you get plenty of cash from my father. Don't trust the telegraph." Her incredulity sounded a lot like James.

My glamorous, birdlike aunt had divorced two husbands and was happily childless. She had aged. She told me with narrow-eyed intent, that she had some money from her last husband and did not depend on her father. She wore store bought frocks in primary colours, she smoked, swore, drank spirits and shouted as she spoke, often breaking into hoarse cynical laughs that came up from her belly, and ended in a rough cough. I had memories of a gentler woman, with none of these tense mannerisms. Marriot booked us both into a hotel so that she was closer to the shops and Lyons Corner house, where she met old friends. She loved to eat sponge cakes with glace cherries, nuts, cream and chocolate. She drank Turkish coffee as thick as treacle from tiny cups gilded in gold. We were both relieved to have female company, although she could not recognise the child I had been, nor I the woman she had become.

Our unremarkable Atlantic crossing was made up of meals and long naps, and occasional slow rounds of the deck. I found an isolated place in the stern to play the violin for an hour each afternoon, and I noticed a handful of passengers came at the same time and sat at a discreet distance, hiding behind their books on a deckchair. Florence did not like the violin.

"You are nothing like your mother," Flo said. "We just had fun. You are a little bit serious."

"I am serious," I admitted. "You would probably have preferred Fanny. She was fun."

"That poor child who died?" she said. "Doesn't sound like it could have been much fun from what I heard."

I wondered what she had heard. Once we reached New York and I wanted to see the sights, Flo could not tell me the location of museums or art galleries and she could not locate any of the city's landmarks on a map or tell me some of its history. She did not walk and found my desire to explore the city on foot, odd, but she was pleased to let me make travel plans.

"My father is paying you to organise me, so you had better do your job," she said.

"Paying me?" I asked indignantly.

"Well. He's given me your bed and board," she said. "You've got pocket money, haven't you?"

I was no longer surprised by what my relations did with my money. Flo was content to write the cheques if I made an itinerary to ensure we had some fun. She had a capacious motor car that was garaged beneath the apartments. She could not yet drive competently. On our journey into Canada the car shuddered and leapt and blew billows of black fumes that terrified me. When we stopped, she searched the stores for anything she could eat while I filled my notebooks with observations, which I dutifully copied into long informative letters to Aunty. Getting the motor going again was a trial. It seemed to me that a motor should not be so obstinate. My aunt's squealing commands were no help, and so I resorted to the book of instructions. While I was reading, a man in green overalls from the gas station came and offered to help me start the motor. My aunt waited impatiently with a cup of tea. The mechanic drove me along some wide-open roads to demonstrate how the vehicle could be made to run smoothly at a cracking speed that we had never reached before. Once I mastered the motor, we took regular excursions into New England in Fall. In winter we made journeys by train, steamboat, and tramcar.

Although I enjoyed our adventures, Florence was a disappointing character. She drank a lot of gin, and she was too interested in herself to be a conversationalist. I realised the rich life of Morning

Lane had spoiled me. Without music, books or causes, we soon ran out of topics. My aunt complained incessantly about small irritations, such as the food, beds, and the weather. Yet she told me I was a reliable companion, welcome to stay at her apartment indefinitely. My domestic skills were appreciated. I made breakfast and simple suppers, and I could turn a bed for her and run to the cleaners.

"You have a very understanding way," she said. "I like having you with me."

Once she tired of travelling – I suspected it was the expense she minded – life was less interesting. There was no elevator, and as the apartment was on the third floor, the climb was so hard on Flo's knees that she preferred that I ran the errands. I enjoyed Manhattan regardless of the temperature because the streets rumbled with life. My walks wound past the river and port and through swampy patches of park. I was certain I was not in the safest parts of the town, but I relied on my physical size and speed to protect me. Staying inside was not an option. The apartment on Lexington Avenue was barren. The apartment had low ceilings, dull lighting, and it was stuffed with modern furniture, with views of rooftops, and not a green leaf in sight. There was no piano, no library, and no history. After our travels ended, I felt adrift again, as I had with my grandfather, except that now my energies ached to be expended. A shift in landscape and geography alone, was not enough.

"I wondered how I would entertain you," Flo said, her face alight with a happy thought. "But you entertain yourself. You are just like me – there is nothing for me in London because my sisters are dead."

"I still have sisters at home," I said. "I miss them."

She sat up in surprise, her cigarette trembling in a long holder. "Sisters? Do you mean that poor mute child?"

"Jess. Yes. And little Pearl."

The moment I mentioned Pearl's name I felt a pang of longing. In my mind's eye I could see her galloping exuberantly about the house. Florence sucked hard on her cigarette, the labours of her mind evident in the twitch of her mouth and the flickering fine lines of her plucked eyebrows.

"Pearl? Was that the servant's child? Wasn't there some scandal?"

"No. No scandal. Uncle Gus adopted Pearl. Her mother had died."

"Adopted her? As an unmarried man! But why?" she asked, offended by the idea. "He never liked children. He was appalling with those two of his own.

We thought he might finish up doing away with them. They got in his way, you know, of his liaisons, and his theatrical life. A man will not generally take on a child, especially one that is not his own."

"He took me in," I said.

"Only until James got home," she asserted.

These words dangled. I thought them over for a long time as she made smoke rings and examined her fine ankles resting on a red velvet footstool. I would not bother her with truth. She was ominously opinionated, quite like Fanny had been, with a unique logic which included rejecting, with invective, all thoughts contrary to her own. I could sidestep most sensitive topics, but she constantly returned to the ones that generated the most heat, such as my grandfather and my uncle ... her father, and her cousin. The more contempt she expressed for them, the more I wanted to defend them.

"Angus sold his soul to those dark churches in Scotland," she said, pulling the subject from nowhere. "What a sad man, having theatrical aspirations and being born into dour religion. It was Angus who gave Helene the money to go off to France to find a singing teacher. My mother never forgave him. My father didn't speak to him for years."

"I think they are good friends now," I said.

She pursed her lips to throw doubt on my words. I returned her gaze with inscrutable goodwill. I knew this benign expression overwhelmed opposition. It was something I had learned from Angus.

"I think you like the old landlord, don't you?" she asked.

"Grandfather is always kind to me, Flo," I said.

"Of course. You are still young enough to think everyone is kind. What about Aunt Caledonia? Is she kind to you?"

"Yes. In her own way."

She scoffed at me. Apparently, kindness was a miserable attribute. My reluctance to give Aunty unconditional endorsement set Flo off. She began with Aunty's chaotic classroom at Cheltenham, the mind-numbing Latin classes that had no relevance to their lives, and Aunty's passionate female friendships. I found I could not sift the truth from spiteful fiction. I felt ashamed of my moral cowardice, but I could not come up with any defence of Aunty without mentioning kindness. I wanted to tell her how many nights Aunty had sat up watching Fanny. How she taught Agnes to read. How many hours she played with Jess. Eventually, Flo said with a little grin of victory: "And they say she had a chap on the side, you know. Some fellow living at the old place in Yorkshire."

"Her cousin Ced," I told her. "I don't think it was scandalous He was just a cousin, her companion who worked there."

"Cousin companions are not always as pure as the driven snow. You know that."

I realised quickly that I was unsuited for a life of leisure with Flo. She felt irritated by the violin, so I went up to the rooftop every afternoon, rugged up in two coats. I did not have enough music to absorb me, and I missed my piano. While Flo exulted in freedom from responsibilities, I felt bereft of real work. None of the letters arriving from home expressed any need of me. I wondered if Jess was getting enough attention. I fretted that Pearl would become the victim of James's merciless tongue unless her intellect became obvious. I wondered whether she was achieving fluency in sight reading her music, turning the pages, getting the scores back into alphabetical and numerical order.

I needed a music teacher, or the use of a piano. I could not rent a piano for a third-floor apartment, and anyway, Flo was not sympathetic. I scoured the newspapers, but I could more easily find work teaching music, than locate a professor. I went cold calling on teachers, but I paid for a few tedious lessons. They asked me to play childish pieces, took my money greedily and said little. I was so unpractised that I was ashamed to mention how much musical education I had.

I went into Central Park with the Gagliano and found a substantial tree to lean against, playing feverishly for an hour. A few people stood in the distance, listening. I was often asked if I knew a little Bach. The appreciation of strangers was gratifying, although Bach made me homesick. One afternoon I heard a prayer form in my mind, and the complete thought escaped to God. I needed a teacher who could move me past the Bach ennui, the morass of fear and the sense of failure and guilt that stalked me because I had walked away from everything of value in my life. I wanted to move on and make something of myself. I wanted to be a musician. I wanted new music. I felt like a tragic, to find myself speaking to God as I fiddled, but I had nowhere to take my anxious thoughts. I recognised, resentfully, that Bach was my comfort.

There was a letter from Aunty waiting for me when I arrived back at Flo's. A scrap of paper fluttered out of the envelope to the carpet, and I put my foot on it as I read quickly through her familiar mundanities, the weather, the spring bulbs on Morning Lane, the girls, until an unusually personal comment added at the end of the letter made me draw a sharp breath.

"...the doctor said Fanny lived twice as long as any child he knew with such a malformed heart. Angus believes your friendship with Fanny kept her alive. I think so, too. He was so grateful to have you in this house for those years. I know he misses you, but oddly, I miss hearing you both play the pianos. You should go on with your musical education. I am sure there will be many opportunities in that wonderful modern city. This is my repentance: I will send you money for lessons if you find a good school. Angus mentioned that he knew a professor of music in New York, and I got the address in case he is still there. I never realised how much music heals the soul, until the pianos in this house fell silent. You should play for your own pleasure Perhaps one day Angus will play for his own pleasure once again. It breaks my heart that he is not playing."

The last phrase made my eyes fill with tears. But then, I remembered the scrap of paper under my foot. It was the address of a piano teacher, in my uncle's handwriting. It was a strange name without vowels, but it was a life raft. If it was an answer to prayer, I would not admit it. The street was only a block away, off Lexington Avenue. I went out again immediately, my long legs striding along the sidewalk with ferocious determination, Aunty's words hammering away: he was not playing. I could not remember a day when he was not at the piano. His joy had gone, and so had mine. How ridiculous that we were half a world away and not playing individually, as though we needed a muse. I had saved him from the tedium of teaching, but music had saved me from my sorrows. Music had bound us in a gift exchange, nothing ransomed. Only musicians could grasp the bond of friendship forged through making music. Angus had no less love for Fanny or Jess in their limitations, not any more for my capacity. He had trained me to the threshold of a concert career he had craved, and I had answered the siren song. Nothing less would satisfy me now. I had run away from all the opportunities that pertained to being a daughter of the house, but the gift was in me. I had to make my own way, find a way forward to become wholly myself: a musician. I had no regrets for the fierce independence that had put me here, in Manhattan, with no option except to navigate my own destiny.

As I approached the street corner, I heard harmonising voices. I had walked past these knots of men before and wondered who they were. Tavern singers? I had glimpsed them leaning into one another, a finger to the ear, creating a syncopated sound. Today I had a reason to slow down and look more carefully. Their crumpled black trousers and greying dress shirts identified them as theatre folk. I was so fascinated by the rhythm of their song that I slowed my pace long enough see a blackened brass nameplate bearing a name without vowels that matched my note, *Hnlczk* and the words *Professor of Music*, attached to the brick façade. I could not even pronounce this man's name if I went to call on him. All along the low brick wall men and women sat listening reflectively to the song, trying to catch the sun, exchanging occasional words. These were foreign profiles, refugees, skull caps, scarves, and occasionally Negro and Spanish faces. The women's cotton dresses were thin and colourless. The sad struggle to stay warm, shivering in shawls and old coats, was evidence of something close to poverty.

"Is there a piano teacher here?" I asked a barefooted girl of about six who was sitting on the edge of the group. I was not confident the adults would speak English. One of the men began to smile wryly and pointed his thumb at the apartment block, upward. I followed the rapid ascent of the girl's thin milky legs through five flights of naked steps. Each time we passed a group of people chatting on the landing she informed them gaily, “Piano teacher.” The thumbs pointed upward, the faces opened out in knowing smiles. I could not interpret whether the gestures were goodwill or amusement. My face burned with the fearful anticipation of negotiating tuition with yet another stranger, just because I wanted to find a piano to play.

The girl showed me to a wide apartment, its double doors open onto the top landing A miniature man in two black coats was living in the untidy space. There was a calico cat draped over an old upright piano. From the door I could see the piano was little more than an iron frame raised on wedges of wood, bereft of all beauty. The little man was rummaging along the edges of a sideboard with both hands, searching for something in the piles of debris. I was about to turn away when the girl ducked around me, knocked, and fled. As the professor approached the door, I saw his fingers were thin with bulbous knuckles of arthritis. His bony frame was distended at the hips and his legs were bowed, as though the shape of the old leather chair at the centre of his room, had adhered to him. His black velvet theatre slippers ended in small bells that tinkled as he shuffled. His slippers continued to tinkle for a moment as he stood silently in his doorway contemplating me.

“Are you the piano teacher?” I asked.

He seemed offended by the idea. As my own eyes adjusted to the poor light, he seemed to be sniffing me, sensing my height, lifting his chin to locate my face. His rheumy eyes swam unfocused in their sockets. The smell of cats, tea and fried food wafted out. I thought he was blind, so I stared blatantly over his shoulder into the disgusting room crammed, paradoxically, with books, newspapers and sheet music. The disorder around the base of the piano stool was so familiar to me that I wanted to run in and sort the scores. I rattled the coins in my hands so that he could be certain I was a paying customer, but still he hesitated, moving his head back and forth to interrogate the light for clues to my identity. His profile was almost feline in its disdain. It seemed odd that a man so poor could dismiss pupils so casually.

“Can you play?” he asked.

“I have passed the Royal Academy of Music licentiate in London,” I said.

“English girl,” he observed.

He was unimpressed. I turned to walk away when he said: “I am not a piano teacher anymore. There are many better places for an advanced pupil.

But…" His pause was marked by a flourish of his hands sweeping up elegantly so that the palm of his right hand held me expectantly, the left forefinger poked towards my face in readiness for the next entry:

"What is your name?"

"Kate Elliot."

"Elliot. Elliot. I taught an English boy with that name. Angus Elliot."

"He's my uncle," I said. "He's in London."

"Ha. I taught him in Leipzig. But now, my eyes are no good, so I don't teach, but I would like to hear you play. Perhaps I can help you find the right person. Let me hear whether you are a musician or merely a nice lady piano player."

He waved me into the grim room with another dramatic sweep of his hand. I went to the piano, and the cat rose up like a majestic ship and padded away. The piano shelf was littered with music from my own repertoire. It was an intoxicating moment. I felt parched for music, and I wanted to slake my thirst. I lifted a score from the top of the piano and shook off the dust and cat hair. It was Beethoven's Piano Concerto No. 4 Op. 58. Then I caught sight of the piano concerto number one by Liszt, and Schumann's piano concerto Op. 54, so I laid them out, only to find Rachmaninov's Suite

No. 2 Op. 17, and Mozart's Piano Concerto No 23, in A major. I greedily examined this harlequin set, wondering if I could make anything cohesive. So many pages were missing or out of sequence. He leaned thoughtfully against a high stool, his eyes searching for me quizzically. My heart was pounding in anticipation.

"I need to warm up," I said. "I haven't played for months."

"Do not make excuses," he said, his hands flowing out again in gracious arcs. I took off my coat and folded it on top of the piano. I sat down and arranged my skirt and set my feet firmly on the pedals. My hands danced over the keys, discovering the peculiarities of the instrument, weaving my way around the worst of its discordance, committing to memory the total absence of some notes. Then I began to play. Within a moment it was as though I was entirely alone in the room. My fingers lost their tension, and a coil of anxiety unwound in my mind. The joy that had been absent from my life for so long, returned in a rush. I could see the joy in my mind's eye, images from Morning Lane - Pearl's lovely roundness flouncing, Fanny dancing, Jess, in a moment of stillness, Angus, always patiently near, hour upon hour, year after year, keeping time with his forefinger as I conquered every new challenge. Just sitting at the piano made me miss them all. I missed the pride and privilege of working alongside my uncle, and him speaking to me as though I was a person entitled to respect. I forced my attention back to the music and refused regrets.

When I had finished the Haydn, the teacher circled a forefinger in my direction, wanting more. I ignored the scores. My hands led me through long movements. Gradually the teacher turned his left ear towards the piano, giving abrupt nods. In my side vision I saw his right hand rising in the choreography of a conductor. Now I followed him. He knew the music in all its intricacies, and he wanted to draw the subtleties for me. He began to urge me, quickening a phrase, drawing me back, showing me the expressive passages in a wordless partnership that went on and on in a timeless vacuum, the room receding, every anxiety washed away in the music. This was so familiar to me that I could have been in the studio of Morning Lane. As the last notes died away and the sibilance of families in the surrounding apartments enveloped us again, he said: "Miss Elliot, you can call me Herr *Ha-nil-shak*. Or you can call me Maestro."

"Maestro," I said, just to hear the word.

"You were not reading notes, were you?"

"No. Did I make mistakes?"

"A few," he said lightly. "Perhaps you got into bad habits. You have such a good memory and that is a danger."

I recalled my months of thunder before I left Morning Lane and admitted that I had been practising badly.

"You cleverly worked that sad piano. Have you always had to play dreadful old instruments?" he asked.

"On the contrary," I said, "My uncle spared no expense on pianos. But every church hall in England seems to have a piano like this, and that is where we performed."

"Why have you not practised lately?" he asked.

"I don't have a piano. I live with my aunt, and she doesn't much care for music."

"Come back tomorrow and play my piano. I can help you a little."

The Maestro began to refer to me as the girl in the red coat, a description supplied by a black woman who lived in the basement of the apartment building. She had told him about my English chignon, the blunt clean fingernails, straight back, a downward cast of my face, no rouge or lipstick, and much younger than he had thought. On the third afternoon that I returned he said the red coat was entirely out of character for someone he regarded as an English lady.

"You are so self-contained and very serious ... until you play the piano," he said. "Then you are a girl in a red coat. There is something in your belly like fire. You have been well taught. So, Angus Elliot became a great teacher? Of course, he still performs?"

I nodded, unwilling to admit the limits of his performances. The Maestro refused to take my money. He wanted company, and he reminisced about great orchestral performances in the mid-nineteenth century, mostly in Russia, and he unfolded his own history and philosophy in vignettes. He had fled a pogrom in the Ukraine in 1888 and left behind a symphony orchestra of 88 men. He repeated these numbers often, as though the significance was obvious. A week later I was thundering through Rachmaninoff, dancing over the sticky keys, when he held up his hand to silence me.

"Listen!" he said.

There were no domestic sounds on the other side of the walls, no evidence of industry beyond the door. I heard a few voices whispering on the stairwell, and the dying sounds of a fiddle.

"What is it?" I asked, "Why is it so quiet?"

"Everyone in this building is a musician. We have travelled a lot together. Now they sit and listen to you, wondering if you will play with us."

The Maestro's graceful hands led me back into the music. I suddenly felt humiliated by the poverty around me. These poor musicians had lived a transient existence to pursue their art. I had played all over London with good musicians. I had the best instruments, the best teachers, the best opportunities, given to me, no fee. Now these men wanted me to play alongside them. The memory of orchestra pits excited my imagination. This time would be different. I would become a different person.

"Levy and Cohen have joined us," Herr Hnlczk observed. "Can you hear the violins?"

I nodded and played on, attuned to the faraway strains.

"Cohen is my concertmaster," the Maestro said. "He is a most discerning musician. He would not contemplate having you play unless he was confident. Come tomorrow and I will invite them into this apartment to meet you."

"If they want to play with me, perhaps I should bring my Gagliano," I said.

His eyes wavered and came to a halt and he took a deep breath: "Gagliano? You have a Gagliano?"

I nodded. "My uncle gave it to me."

"Is Professor Elliot a rich man?"

"No, he's not. The Gagliano was the only thing he valued. He was going to give it to me if I became his concertmaster. But I ran away. More or less."

"You must have been his premier pupil," he sighed. "Why are you here? Was your uncle cruel? Did he beat you?"

I laughed: "No. But I think I got too many advantages too easily."

"Bring your Gagliano tomorrow, and we will all envy you and wonder about the man who gave it to an ungrateful child."

The next day Cohen and a few other musicians came into the Maestro's apartment, and we played. The exhilaration rivalled matinee performances with my uncle's boys in London, even though these men were over fifty and they spoke little English. I was reluctant to play Bach, but Cohen was charming and persuasive.

"I love Bach above all," Cohen said, his voice passionate. "In this music, I can hear the voice of God."

"You sound like my uncle. He says Bach speaks to him."

"Of course. Peace and safety, love and forgiveness." Cohen said. "But now, I want you to play for me. Before the Maestro gets any other ideas, I want you in the orchestra with your Gagliano. We don't need a piano player."

The Maestro's symphony orchestra was playing a series of matinee performances, and they wanted me to fill in for absent musicians. In daylight many of them were working in garment factories. I spent long afternoons practising with Cohen and the Levys.

I was no company for my aunt once the futility of her shallow existence began jangling my nerves. The mixing of a single gin and tonic could consume forty-five minutes. She would not get up to shift the static on the radio. She was always smoking languorously, watching anxiously as a same blackbird tapped at the window every day. The irritation of organising her laundry for a Spanish woman seemed to absorb her for hours. The bitter chasm of her unspent life was tragic. She liked to be alone, and she did not resent my absences.

A month into the matinees I received a small parcel from London, addressed to me in Miss Po's unmistakable hand. Mystified, I settled onto my aunt's pink velvet chaise as she hovered smokily over me. Miss Po had ingeniously cut the centre out of a novel and hidden a clip of crisp English pounds in the book. It was accompanied by a brief note.

"She says that she is retiring, and she wants me to take on Uncle Gus's administration. I think this money is to get me home," I said.

My aunt snatched the letter and read it contemptuously: "She says it is not too much to ask of a girl who has enjoyed considerable benefits, and it would repay your debt to the family. You're here helping me. She should mind her own business."

Florence's pretentious Irish American accent faltered as she laboriously read aloud the rest of Miss Po's letter to me. By the time she finished reading, her voice had moved back across the Atlantic so that she announced indignantly in tight nasal tones, "Let Gus get a new secretary. That man is already managed by so many women that I cannot imagine why you are needed. I want you here."

"But Miss Po was not his secretary," I said. "Aunty was doing the domestic budget and the studio fees. I think Miss Po wants me to manage the electric lights business."

"Gus should do it himself. He got a hundred pounds a year from my father for your keep."

"He bought my grand piano with that money," I said. It was a foolish defence.

She stared at me hard, puffing anxiously on her cigarette, reaching for the gin.

"I'm not getting that much money," she said, injured. "My brother James said you were practically a servant in Gus's house."

"All the girls helped. That's why I can do housekeeping," I said, although only Agnes and I helped, and she was practically a servant.

"If Gus bought a piano for you it sure ain't in your suitcase. More his benefit than yours, I am sure," Flo' muttered.

"I have his Gagliano," I said. "The violin."

"Your squeaky old violin? Is it worth anything, Kate?"

"It's too precious for sale," I said.

"I can't imagine he gave you something that's worth anything," she said snidely.

Any mention of my uncle fuelled her animosity. My own venom was still reserved for James. Florence was reading a letter from James that had arrived in the post. It was his usual cross hatched script. She was absorbed in it for a moment while I considered the fate of the cash I had just received. Finally, she sighed and tossed James's letter onto the coffee table, without comment, her index finger flicking at it to suggest I should read it. I picked it up and tucked it under my arm, with no intention of trying to read it. I read Miss Po's letter again, searching for clues to her real purpose. The entire family of Marriots, Elliots and Parmiters, depended on the income they received from the electric lights company. They had helped my father with capital before I was born, and an army of aunts and distant cousins was still beneficiary. I did not want any of them to lose the little packets of cash that were dispensed regularly by Miss Po. I was, however, anxious to manage my own share. I wondered if this parcel of money represented a change in my affairs. Perhaps I would now receive money regularly. I could save it up and buy a piano. I handled the money thoughtfully. It probably was mine and Miss Po had simply added a caveat for her own advantage.

"Just put that money in your pocket and enjoy it," Florence said wearily, lighting another cigarette, her eyes filled with tears that only indicated her chronic low moods.

"I just wanted to be clear on whose money I would be spending," I said.

"I thought we were spending my father's money," she said. "But now you mention it, I think we have been spending yours."

"Not your money, then?"

"Mine? Good grief, I'm waiting on my inheritance," she said. "I only came to get you because my father paid my way."

"I thought you were on holidays in Greece and your companion left you?"

"Darling, my father will say anything. He wanted you out of his house, and I needed to escape from New York for a while. I had a gentleman who would not leave me alone. Story of my life."

Nothing surprised me, but I did not blame Marriot.

11

Back in the Band

Courtly, immaculately suited, Manny Warner arrived at my aunt's apartment for the cocktail hour. We had observed this ceremony on three occasions but only to greet a new bottle of gin. Now it was escalated to a great tradition, with silver, Bohemian crystal and decanters topped with globulous stoppers. Canapes arrived on a brightly enamelled buffet cart captained by the white-aproned sliver of a Latino woman who had occasionally emerged from the bowels of the building to clean or cook for us. My aunt had been fizzing with anticipation all afternoon until the great man announced his arrival with a rhythmic sequence on the doorknocker. I imagined this man had an interest in my aunt, and she evidently shared that hope. It was several moments before

I realised that this was one of the famous Warner brothers, the theatrical entrepreneurs my grandfather had so frequently referred to with awe. They had promoted Helene's operatic career. Manny's brother Dick Warner was often at *The Eccentrics' Club*, and according to the theatrical newspaper *The Era* he was in the West End theatres every night. My grandfather had been invited to successive birthday parties for Dick, which lasted up to three days, moving between clubs and restaurants until they unwound at Dick's house, *Grenada*, in Stockwell Park Road, Brixton, where festivities limped on for another week.

The man filling our small apartment was not a contemporary of my grandfather. He was much younger, darkly exotic, and he had dined his way to the threshold of corpulence. His wide bronzed cheeks were still firm and full, his curly black hair cropped close to his head. His black eyes were both prominent and hooded, his large nose hooked down, overhanging a moustache with waxed handlebars. He spoke clipped English that defied geography. My aunt was smitten. She had slipped into a short red shantung frock, black satin shoes, and her entire collection of diamonds. Manny Warner rumbled away with pleasantries as Florence shuttled him into our sitting room with its rooftop views, and she hovered solicitously, pointing out the delicacies. He wanted nothing, not even a seat. She thrust gin and something into his tapering fingers. He firmly refused a Havana cigar. His second brother Hugo had died of throat cancer, he told us, probably due to cigars. My aunt quickly extinguished her cigarette and batted at the balls of smoke that curled towards the visitor.

"Manny has come for you," my aunt said in surprise, her voice running up the scale in pique. "The girl in the red coat he calls you. Here she is. This is Kate Elliot."

I remained in my seat, hands clutched firmly in my lap, afraid that if I stood up, I might prove as tall as this man. I had a small glass of sherry which I was drinking on an empty stomach, and I felt both hot and giddy. He began to speak rapidly, as though time was more limited for him than other mortals: "Yes. Kate Elliot, I knew your name of course, the child prodigy. Everyone at the Met' knows the girl in the red coat who plays for the Maestro in the afternoons."

"Do they?" Florence asked, startled. "Well, yes, she is such an extraordinarily tall girl."

"I know all your family well," he told me. "Marriot is in my lodge in London. And of course we had your aunt the great bel canto Helene Parmiter, and her husband who played the piano for her, what was his name?"

"Angus Elliot," Flo said.

"I thought to myself, I should run right over here to see my dear friend Flo," Manny went on. "I should let you both know that my brother, Dick, is adamant that we give you, young Kate Elliot, every opportunity, coming from such a gifted family."

"That is very kind of you," I said.

"I don't care who these Bohemians have playing with them in the smaller opera houses, but if the Maestro wants you at the Met, you must have a contract. This is it. It's all the Maestro asked for, I'm afraid, he's very old fashioned. I can do better for you if you come to Warner's directly and go on my books in London as soon as you are eighteen. They say you are a very good musician."

"Are you a musician at the Metropolitan Opera?" Florence asked me in surprise.

"Only at the matinee," I said.

"This contract needs your signature, Florence, because I guess you are her guardian," he said. "Where were you trained, young lady?"

"It was my uncle in London, who directed my training" I said with relief.

Florence quickly pulled herself upright and tidied her skirts. "Yes, she started learning from my cousin Angus Elliot." She was glowing with pride when she said: "He was the one who played the piano for my stepsister, Helene Parmiter."

"Ah yes, they were on our books years ago at Warner's' Paris office. I recall his name because he still does King's Hall around Christmas. Sacred music. Pulls together a very nice choir. Very popular at that time of the year,"

"But his popular compositions are also doing so well these days," I said.

"Who are these musicians that Kate will be playing with?" Flo asked abruptly. Having signed the contract with a flourish, she was rising to her new responsibilities.

"The Maestro's orchestra. Some of these fellows have done every major show since my partner Grau's time. The bloody Russians took one of the Maestro's eyes, by God. Murdered his wife and children. Anything I can do for you young lady; you know where my office is."

I did not. He pocketed the contract, dropped his glass onto the tray, bowed, and left. My aunt had her hand over her heart, her cheeks scarlet. Then she scowled at me.

"You are a dark horse, Kate. I had no idea you were angling to get into the Metropolitan Opera. You told me you were getting piano lessons from a poor old man. And who on earth said you were a child prodigy? Is that what you told them? I hope you are not going to be a dreadful embarrassment getting ideas above yourself. Helene Parmiter was very arrogant, you know."

"She was very gifted, I heard," I said.

"You need new clothes, and you will not be going to the Met again without me as your chaperone. After all, I am your guardian now. I signed the contract."

Her logic was curiously reminiscent of Fanny.

The next day I followed Herr Hnlczk through the laneway to the side entrance of the Metropolitan Opera. It had been too early for Flo, and in any case, there would be no performance today. The Maestro had just told me I was officially assistant to Konzertmeister Cohen, and I would be needed twice a day for the season.

"How much are Warner's paying you?" he asked

"I don't know. My aunt signed the contract."

"Probably girl wages," he sniffed.

"I don't actually need much money," I said.

He squeezed an awkward grin from the side of his mouth, implying I was a little mad. The heavy door groaned open, and the blinding shafts of sunlight fell on the most imposing grand piano I had ever seen. I groaned, not at the sight of the glorious instrument that dominated the platform, but the scene of neglect and chaos. The Maestro misunderstood me and held up both hands in praise of the piano.

"This is the Bosendorfer Imperial. Spruce. Ninety-seven keys. The extra keys are so you can play Busoni's transcription of Bach's organ work. You have never played such a piano before."

"What a mess," I said, pointing to the ponds of discarded food and tickets.

"Sadly, you have to play the trash that Americans love. Comic opera."

He had missed my point, and I realised he could not see the problem. The piano was coated with a thick film of dust. The velvet hood had been discarded on the bare boards along with thousands of sheets of music. The floor was carpeted with orange peel and brown paper bags, teacups with mouldy dregs, smelly damp coats and umbrellas. On the piano shelf, under a large red brick, there were piles of little notes written on cigarette papers, matchbox lids and cards.

"You will enjoy playing this," he said.

"I thought I was playing with the orchestra," I said.

"When I don't want you, they might have you. A conductor must have a remarkable memory, and you are going to be mine."

Ignoring the scores that were scudding underfoot the Maestro said urgently, "Do not move the brick on the piano."

His feet slid across the floor to find the piano stool and he sat working his arthritic hands up and down some scales as I gathered and sorted the music into piles. I used a handkerchief to dust the piano and worked around his hands, flicking out food scraps and paper clips that had lodged between the black notes.

"These keys will stick with all this dust and rubbish," I said.

"You are not here to be my cleaner," he said.

"I cannot work in a mess. No one would dare put a cup of tea on my uncle's pianos. Not even a handprint."

"Did you admire him?"

"Of course."

"If he taught you to keep a tidy house I should not get in your way."

"Good, because I want to move this brick," I said. "What is it here for?"

"Chits. Very important for wages. I can find a brick but not a chit."

"Chits? Well, I can find the chits. Let me get rid of the brick and I will take care of the chits."

Madeleine was our new show, and the Maestro loathed it. My task was to help him learn the score, notate his intentions as conductor, and think a little about the bowing to discuss later with Cohen. The main difference between what I had done for my uncle and what the Maestro needed, was simply proportion. It was a vast venue, seating audiences larger than any I had known. The Maestro's limited sight was incapacitating by any standards. His memory had failed at the same rate as the vision of his remaining eye. I had learned to anticipate the limitations of older people, and I could work around them as deftly as I found sticking keys on an old piano. I looked out into the cavernous theatre and allowed the fear to consume me and thunder through my senses. Then I shelved all my emotions and played to the empty seats so that the Maestro could learn the score. The singers came to rehearse, and I accompanied while the Maestro continued to absorb the nuances of the music.

Late in the afternoon the stage door creaked open to allow in a blinding reminder of another world, and the orchestra appeared, in pairs and little clusters, often with their sandwiches in a brown bag, with oranges and tea, their violins tucked preciously under their arms, cellos hauled unceremoniously, a double bass on wheels gently manoeuvred into place. A woman brought food for me and pressed me to eat cheese, pickles and meat, stuffed between black bread, the flavours of Prague and Vienna that Angus had craved in London. They set up their music stands and began tuning under instruction from Cohen, laughing, flurries of music filling the room until, imperceptibly we moved towards the hush that heralded a fresh flow in orchestration. The musicians seemed like wizened versions of the boys I had played alongside in London. I was at ease among them, speaking their language regardless of their accents. I smiled shyly and remembered to be a friend.

The Maestro tapped his baton and launched his hands in an arc. He was transformed into a powerful acrobat, his torso twisting with youthful vigour as he drew the musicians together in a rush and reined them back into a vortex. I fixed the Maestro at the centre of my vision and played, blinkered to every other musician. I knew their faces, some of their names, and I would become familiar with the ragged pyjamas worn under their trouser, poking out at the ankles. At first, I was afraid that I was an imposter, an interloper among skilled musicians, but their encouragement was generous. I wanted to rush home and tell Fanny that she could have grown up quite easily, because life was simply more play, more drama, more pretence, and even more magical than what we imagined. And sometimes when I remembered she was no longer with me, I felt free, and hated myself for delighting in the absence of responsibility. Day after day we played to appreciative families, and when they dispersed, satisfied, we were left weary but ready to do it again. We wandered into the street and drank coffee at a caravan on the kerb. It was Covent Garden again, except the musicians were much older men, deemed, by my aunt, safe to escort me home.

A black woman took the Maestro back to his apartment. No one else was permitted to take his arm and lead him. After each performance, I picked up a large brown bag and circulated among the musicians, collecting the remains of their day. They surrendered their rubbish, neatly packed up their music, tidied the stands and seats, and looked to me for approval. There were no teacups on the piano. No orange peels on the floor. The Russians respectfully covered the Imperial in its velvet robes and looked to me for gratitude. They worried over their pay chits, and I assured them of every last cent. They fretted over lost scores, and I painstakingly sorted through the piles abandoned at their feet, unable to grasp their disorganisation. At times they began to mutter about the Maestro and the limitations of his age, his sight, and his memory. I was surprised by my inscrutable silence and the effect it had.

Occasionally, when I put on my red coat to leave, Florence appeared from the wings, smartly suited, proudly parental, carrying a novella she did not read. Florence ran after the Maestro, begging to know how I was progressing. He was non-committal, sometimes annoyed, and I wanted to tell her it was not a children's eisteddfod.

"Herr Hnlczk," she called. "It seems odd that Kate is here all day but never plays the piano at night. Will it always be thus?"

"Yes Madame. The only time we will need her is if Conchinski , the pianist, is too drunk to get out of bed. Or perhaps if I fall, because some fool professor taught the child orchestration."

"Because I have exquisite dresses for her to wear on stage, you know."

I was pink with humiliation.

It turned out that New Yorkers did not love *Madeleine* enough to meet the company's financial hopes, and it closed with only a week's notice. The musicians were relieved. They had enjoyed it, but they were ready for the next thing. They gathered in the late afternoon and began to lodge chits with me which I took to a bleak office in the top of the building, where there was an enormous woman, her body overflowing in sack-like garments. She had a lovely round face wreathed in brown curls, and she sat under a single lightbulb, surrounded by towers of paper. My arrival was a welcome distraction.

"So, you are the girl in the red coat," she sighed. "You are very lovely. So young. Beautiful complexion. They have given you this messy job, have they?"

"I am certain it can be organised much more tidily."

She smiled generously: "I do like your English accent. Of course, it can be organised more tidily if someone with two eyes is willing to do it."

She reached into her piles of paperwork and extracted a brown manilla folder containing typewritten lists of names: Adler, Abrahams, Brusconivito, Braun.

"I need someone - you - to tick off their names every day that they turn up, because it will be much easier for me without these chits. And anyway, I have two Levys and only one contract for Levy. I know they substitute for one another if they get work somewhere else, but it's not allowed. Would that be an imposition to you, Miss Elliot?"

"Not at all. I really do like well organised lists. But can you tell me about the music. We need the full orchestral scores."

"Have you done this kind of thing before?"

"I have," I said.

"Not everyone can get along with these strange old Jews. They are very odd," she said. "And old."

"I grew up with a lot of odd old people in my family."

She laughed.

The week that *Madeline* closed, Conchinski got out of bed and came to rehearsals for the next show, sobered by a lacerating press. I presumed I was out of work. The Maestro handed me the new music and left me alone in the bowels of the theatre to study it for him, and he said he would send down some singers who needed my help. It was another awful comedic piece. I spent three mornings alone in the space where brown linoleum competed for prominence over peeling green paint. One morning a shy apple dumpling of a woman came looking for the pianist and introduced herself as Nellie. It was Madame Melba. Timidly she asked if she might sit down for a few moments to warm up her voice. She confided that her legs were aching, tired from travelling, and she felt intimidated by Conchinski.

"If you just want to warm up, I would be happy to play for you," I said.

"That would be wonderful," she said.

She sat and began to sing softly. Her voice was tense. She was not moving smoothly between registers, her notes tentative. I was surprised to find myself thinking so critically about a great singer, but her vocal chords were troubling her. Angus used to send his choristers for a long gentle walk in the park followed by hot tea with honey and lemon. There was no time for that. She stood up again and stroked her throat anxiously as she sang. I played a couple of problem phrases.

"Ah, you heard me. You have a good ear," she said. "Do you have perfect pitch?"

"Yes."

"You are so young. Have you worked with a lot of singers?"

"Yes, I helped a professor who had a baroque choir."

"What would he do with my scratchy voice?" she asked.

"He did have a technique for making small progressive runs up towards the problem notes," I said.

"Let's try. Can you sing with me?"

I began to sing the contralto part as I played, and she sang against me, her voice gaining strength. Soon her voice was running smoothly up the scale and warmth returned to her vocal cords. She sat back contentedly. We sat for a few moments while she told me about her long separation from her son, and her ache for home and her grandchild. I began to understand the time Angus had spent with the most anxious soloists, listening to the tension that he knew would bleed into the performance unless it was soothed.

"Where is home for you?" she asked.

"London. But I'm not homesick."

"That is good, because everyone here loves you, and they would hate to lose you," she said.

"My privilege," I said.

"Humility is very attractive in gifted people. Don't change."

She picked up the music with an artful smile and began to sing again as I returned to the keys. Her voice was now warm enough to sustain its bell like clarity.

"You have done a lot of singing, haven't you?" she asked.

"My voice was trained for a time, but only because my cousin was ill and couldn't go to her classes."

“Is she a singer, now?”

“She died,” I said.

“How sad. You must do her singing for her, then,” she said.

“But I play two instruments,” I said.

“So do I,” she said. “And we only have one moment in history. You should take your moment, whatever it might be, whatever instrument. You must make music for two people.”

After Melba’s stellar performances, Conchinski celebrated. He tried to get back to his apartment by using the fire escape at 3am, missed his footing in the dark and plunged down four flights of iron stairs, became entangled, twisted his ankles and broke his right hand. His screams of pain ensured that about fifty people witnessed his shame. He was not fully clothed, and he had lost his shoes.

“Having cups of tea with sopranos in the small hours of the morning,” the Maestro blustered, calling me up from the basement.

I laughed aloud: “It was not tea. It was whisky and it was not a soprano, it was a tenor,” I said.

“Oh, my goodness, who would confide such a thing to a young lady?” he said, embarrassed.

“I know about musicians,” I said. “Romance. Passion. It gets into the soul.”

"You must have had a complete education with London musicians," he said darkly. "Now, you must take that great man's seat at the piano. Let us see if the musicians are offended to have such a young girl on that grand piano. I do not have a pianist who can learn as fast as you. None of them have good memories."

It seemed inevitable that this was my moment. I took control of my emotions and sat in Conchinski's place. By the end of our rehearsal, the Maestro was confident that we could complete the season without the great man. His attitude was reminiscent of Angus, presuming that the honour of performing would overcome my technical limitations.

"Tell your silly aunt you need to be dressed like a prima donna, and she will have to sit in the wings and chaperone you every night," the Maestro said. "You will be here ninety minutes before the curtain calls."

My aunt was faint with excitement as she dressed me for my debut. The day passed without her senseless weeping. She was almost childlike in anticipation of the event. She gave me her red shantung gown, and it rustled. I had become so thin that the sash wrapped twice around my waist. When I sat down at the grand piano, I glanced down to see how fine my ankles appeared in Flo's Cuban heels. I glanced up to check which Levy we had that night, and I was struck by the transformation of the musicians. Coiffed, suited, shaved, we were ready to transport ordinary New Yorkers, polished and pressed, into a place of romance, drama, comedy and tragedy, for two brief hours. I was nervous to be so prominently on stage, alone, but my excitement overpowered the introspection of my younger self. I was with friends. A few bows flicked up in encouragement at me, then they fixed their eyes on the Maestro. From the opening bars I knew I had found my place in life. Time vanished and I was absorbed in the performance. I did not experience the dangerous desire for the approval of an audience. I was intoxicated by the act of making excellent music in good company.

12
Orchestration

I could not ignore the Maestro's increasing frailty. His fraction of vision was being eclipsed by disease. It was a topic that he would not discuss, but the orchestra mulled over the problem interminably. He was pedantic in rehearsing single phrases repeatedly, in search of some obscure dynamic, relying on his inaccurate memory of the music. When he was wrong, he would not yield to the musicians' correction. His irritation and frustration were destructive to the unity of the musicians. Although the Maestro refused to believe that he was functionally blind, the men who were muttering away pessimistically knew he had reached the end of his working life. One afternoon the Maestro handed me a baton.

"You have done this before, have you not?" he asked wearily.

"Only for my uncle's musicians," I said fearfully.

"Are musicians in London so very different from musicians in New York?"

By the end of the week, he wanted me to conduct rehearsals while he had treatment on his good eye. His trust was flattering. His affirmation freed me from the haunting suspicion that my opportunities in London had only been the result of my uncle's favour, rather than my capacity. The Maestro's decision to give me the baton, albeit temporarily, needed the agreement of the entire orchestra. First the Maestro called Cohen to the piano and asked him.

"Will you be offended to have a young lady on the box in front of you? Just while the doctor is treating me."

"Maestro, I had not noticed that this musician was in fact a young lady," Cohen responded.

They laughed for a moment and Cohen turned to the orchestra with the same question.

"She is a very tall," one of the second violins said.

"She also speaks very nice English," a cellist mentioned.

"She makes sure our chits are collected and paid on time. This is what we need," the percussionist shouted.

"She can also read her music," a voice from the back muttered. There was a groan of agreement, and then a thunder of applause. Their enthusiasm overwhelmed me. Their laughter and banter seemed to contradict the seriousness of the decision. I was only a girl, and I felt like an imposter. I felt as though I was caught in a foolish game, and I was offended on behalf of the Maestro. Later, Cohen suggested a more reasonable explanation for the unanimous approval of the orchestra. The Maestro's pride was less wounded by a young female on the podium, because I was under his directions, and I would not contradict him.

"Of course you are ridiculously competent for such a young person," he said, his words chosen slowly. "But we will eventually have to replace him with a man who has a reputation. We are humouring him, and we are honoured to have you play along with us for this time."

Recalling Madam Melba's words, I took my moment. When I stood on the podium in the dust stream of late afternoon sunlight, I realised I was adopting my uncle's stance, shoulders back, drawn to full height, gathering the eyes of the musicians with a reassuring half smile, giving them confidence that I did not share. I was acting out my musical education, performing authority to lead them. The violins were busily tuning until the hush descended and I was startled to see dozens of expectant eyes shining at me.

"The intermezzo," I announced.

As the baton rose the music exploded around me. My hands held knowledge of their own, and spun away, unbridled but not untaught. My eyes were searching the music bars ahead of the orchestra, yet I could hear the passages for each instrument before they formed. Adrenaline shot through my arteries and my heart fluttered. By the time I became conscious of myself again I had already swept up a flow of orchestration. I would not allow the complexity to overwhelm me, and I settled comfortably into the flow. I was playing them, they were watching me, giving me their confidence. In the second minute of the piece, I was in charge, swimming with the current. I began to hear the individual instruments, a rest, an entry, and I fell into the symmetry of the music as though this had been my embryonic fluid. I was eloquent, coherent, and authoritative. I had stepped out of my own skin to observe the phenomena. I was not awkward. I was alive. Minutes compressed and time vanished. All my latent energy unwound in that act. As we finished, the orchestra sat in astonished silence for a long moment. They had allowed me to lead them, and I felt humbled.

"That was a good start," I said. "But we have a lot of work to do."

They erupted, laughing aloud and their feet thundered in approval.

The Maestro's good eye did not heal in the next month. He was at every rehearsal, afternoon and night, teaching and correcting, hearing nuances of phrasing that I missed, looking forward to the moment when he could return to the podium. Conducting demanded so much concentration that his presence was a help. It was also such a satisfying challenge that I tried not to think that at any moment I would have to relinquish the baton. During his convalescence, the Maestro's friendship with the musicians flourished, their respect and love had returned, and the tensions of the past months evaporated. The musicians knew they were not waiting for him to return, because his last fragment of sight had simply faded out of sympathy for its lost mate. He was completely blind. In his blindness he became uncertain and fearful in his movements. He did not have the confidence of the born-blind tuners who had graced my childhood pianos, and I had nothing useful to say to ease the situation. He could not find the podium step to mount it, and he resisted help.

Forty-two nights into our season in 1914, Manny Warner came down to the theatre and asked to speak to the whole company. A spotlight was turned on him, and the musicians and singers filed into the front rows of the theatre joking about the view from the cheap seats. There was a tremor of anxiety. The memory of *Madeleine* still troubled everyone. Men worried out loud about whether they had enough cash to pay the rent if the show closed unexpectedly.

"My brother Dick," Manny began. There was silence. The international theatrical agent Dick Warner had safeguarded their jobs for years. Many of them had joined Warner's in Europe or in the far corners of the British Empire when they had no English and only the clothes on their backs. The name was revered because Dick Warner was generous and honest. The musicians knew that despite his English name, he was a Bohemian Jew.

"My brother Dick has sent me a telegram today with instructions that every performer with English papers should proceed to sail home immediately because war is imminent. The Germans are threatening to torpedo English ships. I have been able to organise for all of you with British papers to sail under the American flag. If you remain in New York, you will not be able to sail on our account during conflict. All contracts will be cancelled. They say the war will be over by Christmas, and it will be business as usual. We have had a good season, but it finishes next week. You can all collect your pay and your ticket by Thursday. I am going home. and I urge you all to sail with me. Rule Britannia."

There was a murmur of agreement. No one moved.

"That's you Miss," Cohen whispered over my shoulder.

"It is not me," the Maestro muttered. "I have run away from the Russians, the Poles, the Turks and the Ellis Island authorities, and I am not going anywhere now except to the cemetery."

"Oh, I am staying with you, Maestro. I did not come here with Warner's," I said.

"Yes, of course, you came to stay with your silly aunt, so of course you will be safe with her," he replied. "But there is no work."

"I cannot imagine a life without work," I said. "Isn't there an option?"

"Not with English papers."

"I am sure if you go home Professor Elliot can find something for you to do in London," the Maestro said. "Good musicians can always find work."

"He wanted me to put up a shingle and teach," I said.

Cohen leaned over our shoulders and said, "I will put up my shingle, if this man has a spare room."

"Yes, there are spare rooms. Don't you have a home?" I asked.

"No home. No money. Nowhere to lay my head. No wife or child living."

I looked along the row of musicians and they were nodding and smiling.

"This is how we live," the Maestro said. "Rootless Jews! Wandering Jews, all of us. No homes, just music. Years of travelling with Warner's. Now, no contracts."

The elder Levy spoke for all of them: "It's the truth that the Maestro speaks. Some of us were driven across Russia by pogroms. If you have a home to go to Miss Elliot, it is the best place to be in times of war. You never know when you will be able to get home again. For us, never."

All berths for sailing under the American flag were assigned by the end of the week, and when I did not bother calling, Manny Warner came to the apartment, happily holding up two tickets, as though we should have been grateful. Florence simpered as he brought her up to date on the state of the world, but then she batted the information away with the cigarette smoke, unconvinced. She did not want me to go home, and she was certainly not going, either. Manny turned to me and said: “My dear girl, your grandfather cabled me and made me promise that I would get you out of here and home. You are a minor and I cannot be responsible for you once we sail.”

“I came here of my own volition,” I said.

“But not on your own dime,” he said, as though it settled the matter.

Before I could comprehend the reach of my grandfather’s influence, Florence wailed in protest: “But Manny my dear, her career has only just begun. And now you are going to England as well. We are having such a lovely time. I am sure this trouble will blow over. And where is she supposed to live in London? My father is demented.”

Manny smiled apologetically. “Marriot said there was an arrangement to go to the house of a sick uncle.”

I flinched, sheathing my fury, humiliated to be regarded as a troublesome child, tossed around the relatives. I could not imagine why my grandfather was using Manny Warner as his emissary. He had not written to me in months.

"She cannot be travelling in the company of so many men," Florence said. "I am breathless at her doing that conduction with her sleeves rolled up with everyone watching."

"Of course she needs a chaperone, Flo'. I have booked a berth for two," he said. "I will leave the tickets with you. It's a free ticket one-way for you to go home Flo' and you should take the opportunity."

"I have no desire to go anywhere," Florence said indignantly "It's England's war. Not mine."

That declaration was a relief to me, but there was a problem with money. Miss Po had not sent any more cash, and she had not answered my enquiries. I would have no money of my own, unless I earned it, and all hope of earning had just ended.

"Thank you for your help, Mr Warner. I've enjoyed my time in New York, and it was wonderful while it lasted."

Manny said in a mollifying way: "Wars never last. For these old musicians that the Maestro has collected, this was probably their last gasp. But you, young lady. We will have work for you in London as soon as the theatres open again. Come to our London office and we will find you something."

13
Puzzle Pieces

Dr Stowe walked back into my life while I was considering my options. Her contagious excitement was like an English Spring. She brought news of her journey among America's radical women. Florence had apparently always known Dr Stowe's whereabouts, but her name had never been mentioned. Florence invited her to Manhattan for drinks, unaware of my passionate admiration for this outrageous woman. Suffragettes of America had rallied wherever Dr Stowe spoke, demanding not only the vote but their place in professions and institutions that were controlled by men. They also wanted her knowledge of birth control. Many married women wanted to limit their fertility and family size, but religion was an obstacle. Dr Stowe had fled London nine months earlier with a bevy of leading suffragettes after a round of violence, imprisonment, forced feeding, and the private belligerence of husbands. When she mentioned that Robart was the most prominent male radical still in prison, on concocted criminal charges, and his health was failing, she looked at Florence and me as though we would share her sense of injustice.

"I'm not sure it's right to pour paint over Members of Parliament," I suggested, mostly in the interests of extending the conversation. "It was even reported in the New York Times."

Dr Stowe's eyebrows bristled into an arc of indignation. "You sound like Miss Marriot," she said. "Where would you be, today, Kate Elliot, if your uncle had not been a feminist."

"Well, I'm here now," I said. "I'm here because of Dr Ethel Smythe."

"Exactly," Dr Stowe snapped victoriously. "Dr Smythe is one of our greatest suffragettes. No English father in his right mind would allow the shenanigans that Angus did with you, off on your bicycle to the West End in the dead of night, and all the education he usually only gave to boys. All because of our campaigns for women."

Florence let up a whinny of cynicism: "Angus could never be regarded as an English father in his right mind. The stories I have heard from my aunts!"

"Oh hush, Flo," Dr Stowe said gently. "People change. Don't spoil yourself with jealousy. Anyway, you gave me his address in the first instance."

"Only to help you with voice training. I didn't expect you to fall in love with him. For all the good it did you."

Dr Stowe laughed loudly: "He does me good like a tonic."

The present tense mystified me. I had wanted to question her rejection of Angus, but her words suggested she still loved him. I suppressed a smile at the memory of all the nights Fanny had imagined romantic scenes in which her papa finally succumbed to the charms of this lovely creature. I let her tell stories, without interruption, wondering how she sustained a long-term, long-distance love affair, presumably without Aunty's knowledge. She was more theatrical than she had been in England. Her gestures reminded me of the operatic singers who could not abandon their last role, perpetually posturing offstage. I guessed her enlarged personality was the legacy of speaking in public to great audiences. I tried to digest her storehouse of information as she recited events at a thousand miles an hour. She had brought me a bundle of newspaper clippings with Robart's name in the headlines. He had lost his living. His bishop had denounced him. He was on a hunger strike. She watched my reaction. I could not imagine that fearful little clergyman encouraging women in violent agitation, and my mouth remained ajar for so long that she poked a forefinger into my chin, laughing.

"Is it all still happening? Has it never stopped?" I asked, concerned more for the romance than political action. "I have not heard a word of suffragettes for years."

"Of course you haven't. That was Miss Marriot's doing. We have been hiding at Morning Lane, again," she said. "Miss Marriot became very accommodating, although she likes to scold me. She was unhappy when the police came in the night again. They were watching poor Robart from the time of the fire at his manse, years ago. Do you remember that fire, Kate?"

"Yes, of course I do. The German stove caught light," I said, to enlighten Florence.

"What German stove?" Dr Stowe asked, mystified.

"The heater. Didn't it blow up?" I asked.

"There was an explosion," she said cautiously. "Did Angus tell you it was a German stove. Oh, you poor little goose. I can't believe the stories he told you girls."

"You should not be mentioning explosions when you are in Lexington Avenue," Florence whispered sharply. "Those refugees blew themselves up just down the road only a couple of months ago. Russians. Jews or something, they were." Florence seemed anxious to shut down the conversation, so she waved her hand dismissively to circulate her cloud of smoke and told us firmly: "America is the safest place on earth. You should both stay here with me, stay out of trouble, and wait out this war."

"Wake up Florence. The world is in a lot of trouble, and we all are in it. Miss Marriot said you were always an enigma."

"I probably was. She bored me," Florence said. "So does votes for women."

"Aunty only wrote pamphlets," I said. "About education."

"No Kate, that's another legend you've been told," Dr Stowe laughed.

"She didn't write pamphlets?"

"She was a great feminist leader in her day. She made public addresses. She travelled the country with her educational causes. She was fiery," Dr Stowe said. "She struggled for the rights of women in prison, even women of the night."

Flo' said: "Anyway, I love men."

"I adore men, but why become their nursemaids?" Dr Stowe asked. Her voice was resonant, speaking so forcefully that I felt we were in a public meeting. She looked uncomfortable in her disguise of dungarees that were too large and a man's shirt with a tie, a floppy Panama hat held in place by her headscarf, spectacles that were too large and her thick, fading hair dangling in ponytails.

Tired by discussions, Florence snapped. "So just please assure me that you will take Kate on the boat. It's a free ticket, my dear, and it should not go to waste just because I don't want to go back to London again."

"I am thrilled to be offered a free berth," Dr Stowe said, beaming. "Delighted to travel with Kate."

Once our plans were settled, and Dr Stowe went out into the night, Florence got out a cabin trunk with the evidence of journeys on the Nile – years and years ago, she said - still pasted in a bright collage on all sides. I had so few clothes of my own that she offered me fashionably vulgar garments, too good for an English stage, she said. If anyone should ever invite me to play the piano again, she said dubiously, the frocks would save my money. She lit another cigarette, considering something she wanted to say. She was usually so superficial, but her eyes were brimming with tears as she began to wail, "I don't want you to go. It's like losing you all over again." She wrapped her arms too tightly around my neck and gave me a kiss reminiscent of Fanny's damp affection. All her warm smells were comfortably female, almost maternal, except for the sharp stench of cigarettes and gin that seemed to cling to her clothes and hair. I sat on her bed with an arm around her. I noticed afresh that she was childish, so like Fanny, although she had been drinking steadily for days and so nothing she said was reliable.

"Your mother was my best friend," she said. "I felt like I had got her back again when I met you. We have had such fun together, you and me. New people. The theatre. Promise me you will come back." Her words contained the full weight of her sadness, but I could not promise. Without the company of other musicians New York would have been a lonely place. While I sometimes pitied Florence, mostly I felt frustrated by her isolation. I could not live in a house so devoid of life.

"You should cable James to tell him you are coming." Flo said.

"I'm going back to Morning Lane, to Uncle Gus," I said.

She jerked back angrily: "Why would you go back to that man? He isn't your guardian, James is. I thought you were running away from Gus because he's so cruel and careless."

"No. Goodness no. He has been a good father to me."

"Why did you run away? Girls run away from bad fathers, not good ones. I should know. I ran away from mine. Didn't you tell me your life was a misery ... drudgery...at Morning Lane?"

I could not answer, but she elbowed me for some response. I was irritated enough to spit out the answer: "It was James who made my life difficult. He was a hard taskmaster."

Her cold eyes opened wide, and her mouth formed a tight purse that pressed the feint colour from her lips. I had skirted around the topic of James for the entire year Her memories were unreliable, lacking recent observation. She trivialised his invalidity as though it was a phase.

"James? My brother James is the gentlest creature on earth. He would not harm anyone. He is your guardian. Angus is nothing to you. What on earth has James done to deserve this?"

"I don't want to say," I said.

"There must have been something. Why weren't you living at the Parmiter house with James? That was your home. He came back from India for your sake."

"When people are sick, they change. They pull people into their pain," I said.

She retorted in a voice loaded with contempt. "Sick? James has a bad limp, that is all. How can people pull you into pain?"

I could not explain that she was doing precisely the same thing, wanting me in her small unhappy world, to agree with her and offer comfort where it was not deserved.

"I didn't get on with James. Just like you and Uncle Gus apparently don't mesh."

She pulled away from me, and in her gravelly voice she said angrily: "We did mesh, you silly girl. We were deeply enmeshed for years. You know that."

"No, I do not. I thought you despised Angus. I only know what you have told me."

We both paused, staring down at a glittering ochre bandanna in her hands, until she threw it into the trunk, slammed the lid, and went in search of a bottle of vodka.

"Didn't he talk about me?" she called out.

"No," I said. "Never."

"Never?" she screeched through the doorway.

"No, your name was never mentioned," I said in honest confusion.

Then she shouted over her shoulder with brutal finality and bitter gratification:

"Angus destroyed my life. And I destroyed his."

I was stunned by her outburst. I recognised the classic opera plot in my aunt's words. Only intimacy and betrayal left in its wake a rage that demanded violent retribution. This was not the benign resentment of cousins who had a quarrel. Although I had read her schoolgirl letters at Morning Lane, I could not have guessed that her crush on her older cousin had played out to a malicious conclusion. She had been in love with Angus. This would have been tantalising gossip for my late-night speculations with Fanny. I realised with satisfation that I would have someone to dig this over with. When I had Dr Stowe all to myself, I would get the story.

14

The Eleventh Hour

Dr Violet Stowe transformed herself into the quintessential English Aunt. My Aunty Vee. She came aboard in a tweed skirt, a voluminously flounced white linen blouse with a bow at the throat and flat brown leather shoes. She had the invisibility of a woman in middle age. Her hair had been given such a merciless cut that she was left with only a halo of tight greying curls, over which she fixed a large silk scarf wrapped at her throat. She was exhilarating company after months of Florence's dull patter. Our sea journey was punctuated by political discourse. We leaned over the railings watching the rhythmic swell of the chill ocean. She wanted to know every detail of the events that took me to the Metropolitan Opera. I wanted to know about her turbulent public life among feminists. She rapidly recalled her agenda of votes for the common woman, all work for all women, education, and birth control. She coloured the landscape of injustice with familiar swatches of London life. Dr Stowe described the cycle of privilege where a few accumulated more power and wealth, while there was a downward spiral of those on the margins. For Dr Stowe everything hinged on controlling the size of families. Birth control was loathed by the church and demonised by married women, so she had not persuaded the majority of American suffragettes that they needed dominion over their own biology in order to use their votes productively.

"Angus has a great passion for our cause," she said.

"Really?" I asked uncertainly. "I thought he gave it up."

"He took you to rallies, didn't he?"

"Only to hear the music. Ethel Smythe conducting inspired me."

"Was there nothing else you admired about our great cause for women's suffrage?"

"Our great cause was to see you marry Uncle Gus," I told her. "Poor Fanny always wanted a mama.

Apart from you, the only other woman she saw flirting with her father was Miss Po."

"Miss Po indeed," she said with jarring contempt.

"Are you not friends anymore?" I asked.

"That woman was a thief. She is wanted by Scotland Yard for embezzlement. Surely you heard that James had to step in to the run the electric lights factory. It was just about broke."

I laughed so loud that Dr Stowe scrutinised me for signs of hysteria. I laughed out loud for a long time, with my hand pressed hard to my aching cheeks, while she stared at me with big, mystified, eyes.

"She was the treasurer for the East End suffragettes. She went off to retire in Rouen, on everyone else's money," Dr Stowe said indignantly. "Not very funny."

"My money was in those electric lights," I said, still laughing. "I was looking forward to having my own money to manage."

"Then you will have to work for a living," she said. "Why is it so funny?"

"I was just thinking of Uncle Gus suffering fools gladly. He would not believe she was stealing from him."

"Oh, he certainly knows it now," she said. "They had to sell Parmiter to settle the debts."

"It has been sold! No one told me. Where is James living?" I asked.

"I suppose he went home to your grandfather's."

In the early afternoon the musicians set up music stands on the deck, the scores held secure by clothes pegs, and for an hour I led them through excerpts of our repertoire for the enjoyment of passengers. The prevailing wind carried the sound, and we could hardly hear one another, yet a crowd gathered. When it was too cold outside, we formed a vocal quartet around the piano in the saloon and sang some show tunes, badly, while the Levys and Cohen fiddled. As the sun was setting, Cohen began playing the final section of Bach's Cantata 147 *Jesu bleibt meine Freunde*, and people responded happily to the familiar joyful opening. I began to sing the German words, so reminiscent of my childhood, but the crowd turned away in disgust. I was hurt for a moment. Cohen gave me a sympathetic shrug.

"It's the war," he said sorrowfully. "They probably think Bach was English."

Embarrassed by my naïveté, I sat with a pencil at night trying to recall the translation of the piece Angus had penned for Fanny to sing many years ago. When we played the Bach again and I sang in English, the passengers crowded around and applauded, deliriously happy, and they called for an encore.

"I have never understood how Bach does that to people," I told Cohen later.

"It's not Bach. It's his God. This music is giving their souls food in very confusing times. Music is the voice of God."

"Do you believe in God as well?" I asked.

"Of course. I'm a Jew," he said. "We had God first."

We were vulnerable on the high seas with a war unfolding around us, and no one was certain the American flag was protection. At night passengers took fright at shadows and reported strange sightings. By morning the fear boiled up as people passed rumours and looked out anxiously to the horizon. On Sunday afternoon some passengers requested hymn singing. I played the hymns the children of Morning Lane school had shouted out discordantly each morning, and the mood shifted quietly to calm as the fiddlers improvised. Some of the music was unfamiliar to them, but none of the passengers could have guessed. The hymns distracted us all from an uncertain future. The fiddlers were too old for the army, and they were not confident of finding employment in wartime England, or even of being allowed to live at liberty. The problem of where to stay, how to pay, intruded into all their conversations.

"Is your lady companion going to stay with you in London?" Cohen asked me.

"No. She has friends to go to."

"Surprising for such an unfriendly lady," he said.

"Unfriendly? She's lovely."

"To you," he said. "Not to me."

Tucked up in our bunks at night Dr Stowe's hand reached out for mine in the dark, and it was so small and cool that it reminded me of Fanny in our shared bedroom at Morning Lane. Without my busy musical life, I was revisiting my memories of Fanny often, but there was more pleasure now than pain. I caught myself smiling or even laughing aloud when I remembered some of Fanny's absurd notions. The long illness had eroded her mind in ways we barely understood, and I could not resent any of the pain we all shared in her dying.

"Isn't this exciting, Kate?" Dr Stowe asked. "I hope I have not spoiled things by taking you away from Flo?"

"Flo was not easy to be with," I said. "She seemed to cling to me."

"Yes, she does that. A little alcohol and a lifetime of lies."

"She drinks all the time," I agreed.

"She drinks too much for anyone to help her, not even you."

"Me? How was I supposed to help?"

"I think her father imagined that having you there would lay to rest her regrets about losing her own child."

Dr Stowe's words tumbled out lightly, as though I should be familiar with the narrative. I was bewildered for a moment, then an electric light flashed on to illuminate my mind. The puzzle pieces clicked into place.

"Florence Maud Elliot," I sighed. "Did Florence have that child with Uncle Gus?"

Dr Stowe gasped softly: "Well, yes. I thought you knew. I thought you would have talked this out with Florence. Surely Angus talked to you about it?"

"Florence said nothing. Angus only told me half the story. He said the mother of his child had her own reasons for secrecy."

"The mother is the only one who knows the whole story," Dr Stowe said wryly.

"What do I have to do with Florence's child?" I demanded.

We stared at one another, silenced by the realisation that there was no escape from the unspoken words. They would need to spill out between us, now.

"Oh goodness. Katy, I am appalled," she said. "I only brought this up because I thought you would like to talk about it with me. I know Flo' is not good on the details."

"What does Flo's baby have to do with me?" I repeated.

"Everything," she whispered. "You will have to be very brave. You must be brave," She paused, and I waited, hardly daring to breathe until she said slowly: "You were not your father's daughter. I know people have told you this. It is true. You were adopted."

The shock was visceral. I felt like the ten-year-old child on a bitterly cold riverbank, staring at my mother's sodden sewing box, struggling through a fog to comprehend the symbols around me. I was shattered by disappointment for every half-truth and lie I had heard. The magnitude of deception overwhelmed me. She was telling me with such certainty that I had believed a lie, yet my mind was still grasping for a life raft. Once again, I was drowning in lies and half-truths and misinformation. Who had known? The uncertainties were chasms of betrayal.

I could not reconstruct my life story with the new information. Nothing made sense.

"Please. Someone must tell me. Who am I?" I pleaded, my voice childlike and tragic.

"You're Katy Elliot, a concert pianist who performed in New York at just seventeen," she said gently. "No matter what I tell you tonight, you are the same person who rehearsed Madame Melba, and the same girl who is a darling to all these Bohemian theatre folk. Nothing changes."

"Everything changes," I wailed. "Tell me."

"No. I can't tell you until you promise to hold firmly to the brilliant and beautiful Katy Elliot who had flourished in the most appalling circumstances. Do not stop loving the people who love you, just because of mistakes made long, long ago."

I nodded, already uncertain that I would survive an ocean crossing and a war, and the loss of my family name, but the need to know surpassed all other fears.

"From what I can discover your mama, Maud, was so desperate for a little girl that she risked everything to find you and keep you."

"How does this relate to Flo's dead baby at Abney Park?" I demanded. "Why did all this rumour and gossip hound me all my life? Pearl is adopted and she already knows that. She is not even seven and I am seventeen. Why was I not informed?"

She sat up in her bunk and drew a shawl around her shoulders, using the moment to find palatable word.

"Hold the questions, Kate," she said firmly.

"Tell me," I said.

"Your mama was going to adopt Flo's baby, and I think your father may have agreed, because sisters do that. But the baby died. It was Miss Po who arranged the burial. What happened after that we can only guess, but certainly your old housekeeper was involved. She brought you home. You were a substitute."

"My uncle was involved with all three sisters," I said indignantly. "All three of his cousins. I am furious with him. It's scandalous."

"No, no, no," Dr Stowe said firmly. "Your mother was only ever a friend to Angus. She was the one who suffered the rumours, too. Flo' got away without a taint on her reputation. Until now, no one knew that Flo' had a baby. She pursued Angus for years, particularly when he was widowed. But Florence kept him ignorant about their child. Florence told me that it amused her to have all the relations imagining the worst about Angus. He was totally convinced you were Maud's child, and your father's daughter."

"Was it Colden Bridge and the inheritance that brought it all to light?" I asked.

Dr Stowe gave a philosophical nod: "Of course it was," she said sadly.

She pulled her blankets up to her chin. "I do have a lot of gossip about your Uncle Gus and Flo if you want to hear it. I've heard it from both sides. It was not just a five-minute flirtation."

I did not answer. I turned over to go to sleep, but instead, cried hard for ten minutes. Finally, I sat up, ready to hear the story. She described the nineteen-year-old Florence Marriot, feisty and flighty, who resolutely pursued Angus. She was a beautiful but vacuous girl whose love he did not want, but did not refuse.

Florence had argued with her father over something trivial, and she ran away to Parmiter, where my mother, Maud, dispensed unconditional sympathy. Within the week Florence recklessly took the train to Scotland to visit Angus in his parish, having borrowed money from Maud and sworn her to secrecy. When Florence arrived on Angus's doorstep, he was too lonely to turn her away. He was friendless, and her youthful energy revived him. He had never considered Flo' as a suitable partner, and they had never been together, alone. He had studied for a dozen years to become a minister of the Church of Scotland, with higher degrees in musicianship and theology. He had the pastoral care of surpliced choirs in several parishes near Glasgow, as well as ministry to his own small congregation. He spent long days in meetings, visitation, composing and teaching. Every controversy in the congregation swirled around choirs, organs and the singing of psalms, and Angus felt he was just a hireling, the spiritual nature of his calling unappreciated. Every sermon was debated vigorously for a week and every fractional inaccuracy in conveying strict doctrine was critiqued by elders, with long meetings to discuss finer points of theology. He was always alone in a candlelit kirk house where the cold nights were endless.

"He never turned people away from his door," Dr Stowe said. "He regarded it as the worst decision of his life that he opened the door to Florence."

Florence did not remain in his spare room for long. Soon they were sharing a bed, living in sin. Angus never guessed at the vigilance of the parishioners who walked along the lane beside his cottage, making a covert inspection of interesting items dangling from a makeshift washing line. Six weeks after Florence's arrival, the Presbytery called Angus to account for the young woman living in his house. Like a man waking from a bad dream, he realised he had shattered the trust of so many and ruined his vocation. Worse still, his affection for Flo' was self-serving, opportunistic, and ephemeral. He did not lie, he did not repent, but he also refused to marry her to atone. He was dismissed from the parish, a hasty end to everything he had worked for. His case was referred to Synod, which could either appoint him to another parish far from the scandal or end his ministry entirely. He was still regarded as an outsider among the Calvinists, not even a Scot despite his ancestral roots in the fishing clans. He was the product of a strict group of brethren who were regarded as Arminian heretics, wildly apocalyptic. With no income and no home and Florence refusing to go back to London without him, the couple stayed in a lice infested room in a cheap pub in Dumfries until his stipend ran out. Eventually, they had no choice but to telegram Maud, and she sent them the money to return to Parmiter.

The year 1897 was made memorable in our family because most of the relations had a stake in the new public company that my father, Coates Elliot, launched. When he went abroad to set up his trading networks, he wrote back to everyone with exciting investment options and promises, and the relations passed around the reports of his travels, anticipating future profits.

With Angus and Florence due to return, Maud let the staff go to protect her privacy, leaving only the seamstress, Dotty, whose criminal record made her unemployable. One chattering maid quickly found a new place in a Marriot household. This was an alert to some of the aunts that something was brewing with Maud. My father probably imagined that Maud was sitting in the parlour with her sewing, taking walks in the park with her sister. Instead, Florence was hysterical most days, begging Angus to make a future for them together. He was depressed, engulfed by shame and grief as his immorality case plodded through Synod.

Angus knew he needed to get away from Parmiter quickly, because Marriot or the aunts would inevitably come calling. Marriot had paid for Angus's long education in divinity, and he had taken great pride in his ordination. The simple solution to the immediate crisis was to find Angus work. Maud sent a telegram to her step-sister, Helene Parmiter, who was performing with a Viennese opera company that needed musicians. A week later Angus was at Warner's International Paris office to sign a contract.

Helene and Angus had not seen one another for ten years. Their young love had been blighted by the conditions Angus had devised for their marriage. Influenced by dissenter quarrels over popular entertainment, and supported by Mrs Marriot's strictures, he told Helene she would need to be content to sing in church once they married. When he arrived in Paris, with the church bolted behind him, and hours of romantic arias ahead of them, there was no hesitation. The long-deferred passion was rekindled. They decided to marry quickly, and they returned to London briefly between contracts for a private wedding.

"What happened to Flo?" I asked.

"She was having the baby in Bournemouth."

"He completely abandoned Flo," I said, disgusted.

Dr Stowe put her finger to her lips to hush me. "He did not know. Florence did not know because she thought you had to be married to have babies. Maud noticed the bump."

"Poor Flo'," I mused.

"Indeed. When Flo's baby died, she just went back to her father's house heartbroken and unable to say a word, and when she went back to Parmiter at Christmas, there you were, a little redheaded infant. Only your mother knew the whole truth, and I presume, Dotty."

Her voice was apologetic but when I said nothing, she continued.

"When Marriot finally found out ten years later, he could do nothing without sullying reputations."

"How did he find out?"

"It was all Dotty's doing," she said. "She became very senile after your parents died. She told Marriot that you were Flo's child. He had heard rumours, of course, but nothing about Flo'. I think Dotty wanted to be sure that Marriot took responsibility for you. And then, of course, he came to New York to get the truth out of Flo'. She had to revisit the whole horrible episode to assure your grandfather that her own child had died, and she was in an unmarked grave at Abney Park. It sent Florence back to her gin, having her father on her doorstep demanding the whole story. Marriot went home a broken man. All the young people he had educated, clothed and housed, and his servants, had colluded in such an epic deception: Maud, Angus, Florence, probably Coates, certainly Dotty, and of course, Miss Po. Everyone betrayed him. But by the time he found all this out, he really enjoyed your company. He firmly believed Gus was your papa."

"Even Fanny thought Uncle Gus was my papa," I mused, disappointed because the pretence had been so comfortable.

"Kate, the cottages of England are full of children who are not their father's sons and daughters. The only important thing is that children find someone who cares for them Your mother adored you. Angus loves you like a daughter. Sadly, I can't imagine how your father fit into all this. He was thoroughly deceived, I think."

I began to feel a pang of grief for my father. He suffered years of humiliation, never free to explain or excuse or defend nor silence the innuendo that he had been cuckolded by his own brother. My mother's manipulation was a legacy of love, still reaching out to reassure me that I was a wanted child. As for the three sisters and their conflicted affections for their cousins, it was the most unbelievable farce, and I wondered if it could be set to music.

Dr Stowe's voice went on, musing over details that could never be resolved. I quickly fell asleep. Something had shifted in me that redefined my place in the world. My musical gift was not a mystical legacy or inheritance but something my uncle had laboriously nurtured in me, because I had wanted it above all else. It was my wellspring of joy and my destiny. I regretted the love lost between me and my unhappy father, but I no longer blamed him. Of course he had known. He trusted Miss Po and my mother was outside that friendship. Secret knowledge was power to Miss Po. Coates Elliot had kept me at the edges of his world, visiting his suspicions on me in all the simmering tensions with my mother, whenever I slipped down the stairs to remind him of my presence. Angus was not my father, but he had certainly atoned for my father's failures. The most curious aspect of my new story was that I had no idea where I came from, yet nothing had fundamentally changed.

Nothing could diminish me now, because I was Miss Elliot, the pianist who had made her debut at the Metropolitan Opera. I had rehearsed Madame Melba and served for a season as personal assistant to the great Herr Hnlczk. I felt invincible. I was also adopted.

15
The Landlord

I awoke with a plan. I would take the homeless musicians to Morning Lane and test the magnitude of Angus's principles. It had always been a house full of strangers, orphans and aliens. He would not deny these men a bed. They were musicians, and he would make them doubly welcome because they were Jews. It seemed outrageous, but no more fantastical than suffragettes, orphans and corrupt clergy in need of a safe house.

"It's a big house, and my uncle always needs good musicians. He conducts all the baroque and classical music that you know," I assured Cohen.

"But we are Jews," Cohen said solemnly.

"He will like that."

"No Miss. You do not understand. We are Jews. Foreigners. People think we are not good."

"But my uncle thinks the Jews are part of his religion. You can ask Dr Stowe, she will tell you about him."

"Your chaperone? I am certain that she does not like Jews."

I glanced across to the far corner of the deck where Dr Stowe was staring out to sea. She always drifted away from me when the musicians came on deck. When they began to play and draw a crowd, she went below deck. I thought she disliked theatrical music, but now I realised she did not want to mix with the men.

"But you're in the bible," I said. "God's chosen people."

"We are, yes we are, my dear Miss Elliot," Cohen persisted patiently. "But we eat strange food and have strange habits. No English gentleman will want us in his house during this war, even if he is a very exceptional musician, very kind and very rich."

As far as he was concerned, the matter was closed. On the final evening of our voyage Dr Stowe sat at tea with me. She had been playing patience most of the afternoon and she was glad to have my company. I noticed that her mother's amethyst rings had been moved to her wedding finger. She had so many subterfuges. I thought this one was to discourage men.

"You will be home in your own little bed before you know it," she said. "I hope you will not be too unkind to Angus for his sins of omission."

"How many suffragettes hid at Morning Lane last year?" I asked.

"Ten, actually. Chaos. The two Marys were in the bed with all Fanny's cats. One of them had kittens ... the cats, not the Marys. Jess bit one of the ladies. They had been more afraid of being bitten by the cats," she laughed. "Why do you ask?"

"There are ten musicians with nowhere to go when we get to London. I would like to take them to Morning Lane, if they will come."

She turned quickly to study the rabble of musicians on the deck, chattering in Yiddish. Her eyes travelled over their shabby old suits. Sotto voce and with a deep sense of alarm she said: "They are Jews."

"Do you despise them?"

"No. I'm a feminist. We are egalitarians. But it's wartime and they could be arrested as enemy aliens unless they have proper documentation? Where do they come from? Do you even know what side they are on for this war?"

I felt so naïve, so immersed in music, that I had not considered politics. For musicians, the war was just an unwelcome disruption to our program. Members of the orchestra seemed to speak many different languages, German, Russian, Slavic languages, and fractured English. They had lived in Prague, Vienna, St Petersburg, Leipzig and Amsterdam. I suggested to Dr Stowe that she come and ask them her questions, but she took my arm and drew me away to the far end of the deck. Her head was closely covered with the same silk scarf that had protected her from the sea breeze all week, her face barely visible. Her head was downcast as she paced thoughtfully, pulling me close each time she wanted to clarify a point. Were they political? Did they have any family in England? It seemed that she genuinely wanted to resolve my dilemma, and she stared down into the deep waters for a long time, pondering the problem of the ten musicians.

"Here we go again," she said. "My Lord we have landed in such dangerous waters. Katy, darling, you are so clever in many things, but not politically."

"I certainly never knew Jews were such a problem."

"They are not the problem. It's me. I am the problem. I am a major problem to your ten musicians."

She saw the perplexity in my eyes and pulled me closer as she adjusted the scarf tight under her chin.

"Don't you understand that I am an anarchist. Flo was right. Since the Lexington Avenue explosion none of us are safe. That bombing was the work of Russian Jewish anarchists. In the eyes of any government all anarchists and all Jews are the same. I cannot be seen with them."

"I don't even know what that word means," I said. "Anarchists?"

"Remember we mentioned that fire at Robart's manse, so long ago? You thought it was a German fire exploding. That was me – it was one of my bombs going off. I can handle explosives much better these days, but I almost killed Robart and a group of suffragettes. I was the bomb maker for the suffragettes because I had a science education."

"A bomb," I repeated, my breath caught with excitement and horror. "I wish I could tell Fanny. That is the most astonishing and appalling thing I have ever heard. A bomb maker?"

"Poor Angus was so shocked that I had started making bombs, without him, of course He had you girls to think of. That bomb was intended for the Prime Minister. I was only convicted and imprisoned in England for blowing up letter boxes. Where did you think I was all that time?"

"We thought you had fallen out with Uncle Gus."

"Never. But that is why I am not allowed back into England. Imagine how it would look if I was caught now, an anarchist sailing in with ten Jewish fiddlers with England at war. I want to help them, and I am thinking about what I can do, without getting them all hanged."

"How can you get back into England? Are the police looking for you? Is that why you are covered up and disguised?"

"Don't worry, Kate, I've got Flo's papers. She let me have them with her ticket to take you home."

I looked into her handsome, craggy face and saw that she enjoyed deception.

"I never really knew you," I said. "We thought you would be such a lovely mama. You really are not mama material."

"This is a better life, Kate, believe me," she said. "And look at you. A professional musician, working with these men, and they respect you."

"I did not plan any of this."

"I think Angus did. This is the life he wanted – the life he had once for five minutes. You cannot imagine how much people admire you. Music has helped these people on board the ship to forget their fear, and it has made this journey memorable."

"Do you think my uncle will take these men?"

"You know him, Kate, he can't say no. We will separate at the docks. I will vanish in Liverpool while you take the men onto the train to London. I will send Angus a cable. Of course, you should take those men to Morning Lane. I will ask Angus to meet the train."

We passed the British Grand Fleet at exercises in the Atlantic. The dark profiles of the dreadnoughts moved across the horizon as navy blue clouds rose like an impenetrable range of mountains. We reached Liverpool early on October 31 with a wind whipping the sea into deep stairs that our ship plunged down recklessly until the docks came into view on the estuary, more elegant than anything we had left behind in New York, modern and littered with shipping. We finally settled, lashed firmly against the dock. Dr Stowe kissed my cheek by way of farewell, and held my hand as she whispered: "What is the first thing you will do when you get home?"

"I'm going to take the train to Colden Bridge."

"Oh, goodness, what a strange answer," she laughed. "My question was just an opening to ask you to give Angus a kiss from me. Isn't Colden Bridge halfway to Scotland? Why go there? It can't be a happy place."

"I have to say goodbye to my family. I want to sing to my parents and my brother, and then I will never look back again, as long as I live."

She kissed me again, and asked: "Is that an English tradition?"

"I don't know. I heard Uncle Gus singing over Fanny's grave. And then Madame Melba told me the same thing. If people die with their music still inside them, someone else must sing for them," I said.

She squeezed my hand and left me. I joined the pulsating mob of musicians, actors, acrobats, operatic singers, all noisily and excitedly carrying suitcases, instruments, props and wigs to the train with someone from Warner's calling out names, handing out tickets, providing sandwiches for the journey, so that we travelled on untroubled, on English soil. When we reached London, our musical instruments were stacked on the platform along with trolleys laden with theatre props. The luggage was a small mountain. Some musicians sat on the cabin trunks, and I heard my uncle's name whispered among them, along with the words *Maestro, Christian* and *Socialist*, all of which I had used liberally in my reassurances to them.

Performers of every description wearing Warner's agency brown tags bounded along the platform to friends and families. The reunions were noisy, peppered with Cockney. The men behind me were more thoughtful characters. These humble men with sparse earthly possessions in leather cases held together with belts, milled about me at a discreet distance, discussing their worries with one another. We looked out into the wheat field of humanity, dense clusters of families shifting about as though driven by wind. I wanted my uncle to appear quickly, before my confidence vanished and the men thought better of the plan. Uneasy after Dr Stowe's disclosures, I had double checked their papers. At the behest of Warner's, they had all become naturalised seven years earlier, before they went on tour. When I was confident of their right to remain in England, I worried about their finances. I recalled how their hats and violin cases mysteriously filled with coins each time we played on deck for American travellers, and I wondered if the English would be as generous, because the men needed money now. I was reassured by the thought that in the worst of times people needed music. If I could keep a few musicians together, I had the bones of an orchestra. There were halls in Hackney where we could hold subscription concerts. My grandfather owned some of them. Music could make money. It had paid the rent on Morning Lane.

A sudden clamour of voices made me glance up from my anxieties just as a bare headed man, laughing under a load on his back, came towards me. He was followed by railway porters with empty trolleys. A silver Homburg rolled towards me on a bluster of wind, followed by the unmistakeably rotund figure of Pearl, taller than I remembered, her ringlets bouncing, her own hat clutched against her chest as she chased the Homburg. She stood up in front of me and stared up without recognition. Aunty followed, limping along on her arthritic knees, a shrivelled figure in her best green satin and crepe garments, her white hair rolled in neat bundles under a sepia picture hat. Agnes looked ordinarily herself, in greying whites, unable to contain Jess who wanted to clutch my uncle's coat. It was only the laughter that identified Angus. His long youth was over. The auburn mane had gone. His face was like a loosened drum skin, with thin jowls and drooping eye sockets, although he was heavier around the middle. He might have been a man in trade rather than a professor of music, because there was nothing flamboyant about his appearance. He had not escaped grief. It had punished him. I had an impression that it was Fanny on his back, and I shook myself impatiently into the present and looked harder. His elbows were hooked under a small shape that was neither luggage nor child. It was James. I felt a flash of jealousy, resentment rising like bile. He had wheedled himself into the circle of my uncle's beloved friends. He was pink and cheerful and when he caught sight of me, he raised a clawed hand. In the next moment I was swept up by their chorus of greetings and questions.

"Look at you," Angus cooed musically, "A lady. I am going to give you a squeeze, Kate, you owe your old uncle a little squeeze."

He lowered James to his unsteady feet, and as soon as his hands were free, I stepped into the circle of his unbridled affection. Pearl was hiding behind him, peeping up at me. The whiff of peppermints filled me with nostalgia. I took my uncle's cool hand in both of mine and stroked the fragile flesh.

"I have missed you, Kate," he said. "Something cruel. We must have talked a lot of music. I kept looking for you to hear something I was composing, and I had no one to tell."

"Yes," I agreed. "Every time I had some problem with the meaning of life, I could have done with a diatribe from you."

He laughed again. There was a clatter of applause behind me. Angus caught sight of the musicians over my shoulder. They were loudly approving our affectionate reunion. Angus was making a mental note of the instruments. He stepped past me and extended his hand to the musicians, and one by one they removed their hats and caps and bowed slightly.

"Shalom."

"Shalom."

"Do we have some spare beds?" I asked him.

"Do you realise 55 Morning Lane is not his house, Katy?" Aunty said as she shuffled up to me to take my hand. The musicians cheered when we embraced. "It's James's house these days. We are all living together. A much more economical and efficient way to live. We have only ever paid rent on the place, anyway."

"I am now officially the landlord!" James chirped.

Everyone laughed, except me. I caught a painful glimpse of his frail body, standing uncertainly, his arm resting on Aunty's elbow. He was more twisted than ever. I could not even greet him with warmth. Angus exchanged names with the musicians and helped them load possessions onto the handcarts. Jess came and stood stiffly alongside me. I smoothed her hair, looked into her eyes and kissed her forehead. As she recognised me, she rested her face against my shoulder. Again, the men gave a little cheer. Finally, I turned to James, who was still smiling but unable to shift himself towards me. My own physical paralysis was anchoring me to the past. I knew that I had to step out of history and into my future. I went to him and picked up his right hand, too limp to shake, so I kissed it. The applause and cheering from the musicians delighted him. His grip tightened around my hand and his eyes held mine insistently, in an odd apologetic expression that made me realise he had no control over the contraction of his hand. As I allowed myself to see him, I was shocked to realise that he was still young.

"I'm happy to see you, Kate," he said. "Home safe. I do the worrying. Gus does the praying."

"Have you been well?" I asked him. He was more like the man who had been my mother's darling brother, Flo's brother who could do no harm, and Aunty's Poor Jim. He leaned towards me and said hoarsely: "My life has never been better. Gus insisted I move into Morning Lane because I wasn't managing stairs at Parmiter. Fancy having a bloody hydraulic lift in your house. We all used to think Gus was mad, but that bloody lift has changed my life."

"You seem so well," I said. It was an unreasonable word to use when he was crippled beyond help, but there was health in his eyes.

"Yes. Things have changed for me. What about you?"

I nodded. "Changed," I said.

He had something to say, and I sensed the urgency. When he found the words, it was like a balloon going up, the past evaporated: "Kate, somewhere in my life I forgot how to be friends. I forgot I needed friends. Can we be friends?"

I nodded and said with regret: "We were such horrible little girls. I'm sorry."

"But you were just little girls. Anyway, I always hated teaching school," he admitted. "Are you bringing these musicians to Morning Lane?"

"I couldn't ask that of you," I said.

"Why not? You just asked Gus. Same house, just the other uncle."

"But it's your house now."

"I only need a room and my dinner," he said. "My father has given me the lease, so I get the room for life. He intends the place to come to you, freehold. You've made it into his will. Not everyone does."

In my side vision Aunty was plumping herself up like a rooster, so smug she would have crowed if she could.

Angus reached towards the last outstretched hand and said: "Yes, you must come to Morning Lane. It's a safe house. If we don't fill the house with people that we like, then someone at the war office will fill it for us. Please come and stay."

"How many musicians?" James asked.

"Ten," I said.

"Plenty of room."

About the Author

Annie Woodward was born and educated in London, where she worked as a journalist. After she moved to Sydney, Australia, Annie earned a PhD and lectured in universities for 20 years. When her children began to leave home, she bought a remote bushland property where she could focus on her writing, with alpacas and a colony of calico cats to care for. Her passion for history and genealogy led to research work in archival sources, from which she has published extensively in the academic domain.

I hope you enjoyed reading my story and, if you have a moment to spare, I'd be very grateful if you could leave a short review. They not only help other readers discover the kinds of books they want to read, but they also help support independent authors like myself. I read every review - they really do make a huge difference.

For readers from the USA and the UK, I've set up easy links below that will take you direct to the Customer Review section of Amazon in your particular country.

FOR **USA READERS**, CLICK HERE OR SCAN THE QR CODE:

FOR **UK READERS**, CLICK HERE OR SCAN THE QR CODE:

Acknowledgements

Grateful thanks to my encouraging first readers, particularly GB, a celebrated author in his own right, and my lovely colleague JV.

Printed in Great Britain
by Amazon

60195043R00170